EMERGENCY ROOM

Also by Caroline B. Cooney:

Flight # 116 Is Down

The Stranger

Twins

Wanted!

EMERGENCY ROOM

CAROLINE B.
COONEY

SCHOLASTIC INC.
New York Toronto London Auckland Sydney

No part of this publication may be reproduced in whole or in part, or stored in a retrieval system, or transmitted in any form or by any means, electronic, mechanical, photocopying, recording, or otherwise, without written permission of the publisher. For information regarding permission, write to Scholastic Inc., 555 Broadway, New York, NY 10012.

ISBN 0-590-45740-3

18   1 2/0

Printed in the U.S.A.   01

First Scholastic printing, June 1994

EMERGENCY
ROOM

THE FIRST HOUR

THE CITY
6:00 P.M.

The beautiful Gothic stone dormitories in which the college freshmen lived were surrounded by a very high but equally beautiful black iron fence. This was to keep the City out.

Jersey let herself into the quadrangle with a key. Inside, the landscaping was cool and green. Immense old wooden doors, heavy as coffin lids, led into the Commons.

Four weeks before the end of freshman year, and Jersey was still in awe of the campus. Still thrilled that she was here, attending the best college in the nation. Her father had graduated back when the school was all men, and she had been brought up on his college stories.

Jersey went to her mail slot, opened it, and found a letter from home. Jersey loved mail. Going to college was worth it just for the mail. She ripped open the letter, which had only one word. ENJOY! said Dad's handwriting.

Wrapped in his letterhead was a hundred dollar bill. Jersey laughed to herself. Dad was so tickled that his little girl was attending his alma mater. All year long he had been celebrating by sending money.

Ooooh, goody! she thought. I'm going to get those shoes Mai found at the Downtown Mall.

Mai was one of Jersey's two roommates, a serious competitor for World's Best Shopper. While lesser shoppers found nothing in any store, Mai zeroed in on terrific bargains at every counter. And Jersey's other roommate, Susan, had unbelievably good fashion sense. Susan could take some repulsive orange-and-turquoise scarf — not fit for a preschooler's bath towel — pair it with just the right shirt and necklace, and make herself look like a million dollars.

Jersey's proud father was under the impression that she was enjoying classes, boys, dorm life, and the coast — and she was — but better than anything, Jersey enjoyed shopping with Mai and Susan.

Unfortunately, Mai and Susan had labs on Mondays and, being dedicated future research scientists, would work right through dinner. Shopping alone rots, thought Jersey. Who cares about shoes unless Mai and Susan are along to giggle and criticize and compare?

The hundred dollars burned, dying to be spent, frantic to be exchanged for shoes.

Jersey, Mai, and Susan had become a trio so tight they hardly bothered with other close friends. Jersey left the quad, wandered through the Arboretum and detoured into the library, hoping to spot a shopping partner. She knew nobody well enough to ask them along.

She knew she should wait until she had company. Not just because shopping was only fun with friends, but because of the City. They were always being warned about the City. Always being told that they were not street smart and must be careful about where they walked and when.

Jersey, however, could work up no interest in the City.

Only in the mall.

The hundred dollars was a single bill, but it lay heavy and demanding in her tiny pocket, as if it could not, *not, NOT!* wait for tomorrow.

Jersey keyed herself out the high black gates, and left for the Downtown Mall.

It was the eleventh of May, but already the weather was sweaty sticky, disgustingly hot. The temperature should have fallen by six o'clock, but it hadn't. The Downtown Mall would at least be air-conditioned, which Jersey's dorm wasn't. Generations of important male undergrads had perspired in that Gothic hall and nobody was going to tamper with history and put in air-conditioning.

Jersey hated going to the college dining halls

by herself, or having to stand with her full tray and scout through the room hoping to find a dinner partner. If she had to eat without Susan and Mai, she would rather buy something at the Food Court in the Downtown Mall. Now, along with shoes came visions of Mexican food, twice-baked potatoes, pizza slices, and Heath Bar Crunch sundaes.

Jersey's body was her friend: It allowed her to eat anything any time and stay petite.

Jersey's skirt, shirt, stockings, earrings, and ponytail bow were black, the color of choice on her campus. In fact, the shoes she was dreaming of now were also black; they would be her ninth pair of black shoes.

Within yards of the gate, the City began. No more huge old trees to soften the heat. No more landscaping and bright blooming flowers. No more laughing young people swinging book bags from their shoulders.

The sidewalks were cracked and buckled. The fire hydrant was broken and the stunted tree in its little wire enclosure had died. The pavement generated its own heat, as if there were a contest — City versus sun — to see which could get hotter.

She sweated. Jersey hated sweat unless it came from an acceptable game. Tennis sweat was okay. Street sweat was not.

She passed a brick building with inner and outer bars on the windows and an ugly thick grate drawn across the big wooden entry. The first few months of school she thought it was some old-fashioned jail — it was a church.

Spray-painted on its walls were the initials of the biggest local gang, KSI. On this street alone, according to campus rumor, there had been over thirty drug arrests last year.

But that, Jersey was sure, was by night. This was daytime. Behind her, newly cleaned dorm windows sparkled and the spires of old college buildings glinted in the relentless sun. She was one block from Peppi's Pizza, from which she and Susan and Mai ordered constantly. The City was famous for its pizza, which Jersey found weird. You could be famous for your museums or your theater — but your pizza? What kind of claim to fame was that?

Cars were so tightly parked there was barely room for a line of moving traffic. Indeed, this afternoon, the traffic was not moving. Cars idled, revving their motors, honking their horns, waiting for the lights to turn and the gridlock to cease. Jersey stepped around a huddle of black plastic garbage bags which were blockading the sidewalk like fat angry people.

She was vaguely aware that she was walking past some real live angry people, but Jersey was thinking about shoes. When she looked up she didn't glance at the people near her, but through them, and higher. Three blocks away were the glass spans of the Downtown Mall.

Fashion displays filled the windows, as if amazingly thin, rich people were partying up there.

Beside her, traffic advanced. One car did not move ahead. People screamed obscenities at the driver. Vaguely, Jersey thought of taking a taxi back to the campus. It probably would have been better to take a taxi *from* the campus. But you couldn't let fear rule your life.

No, thought Jersey, smiling to herself. Shopping rules.

The gunfire began.

Jersey did not realize there was shooting until she was flung against the pavement. Even then she thought somebody had pushed her. It was such a great force. A football tackle, maybe. She did not realize that a bullet had shoved her down until she saw her black clothes turning red.

Very red.

As if she had suddenly decided to dye them scarlet.

The body that had never let her down had been punctured without her permission.

I have to stop the bleeding, Jersey thought.

She tried to tighten her hands on the wound, make her own tourniquet, but her hands simply lay there on the sidewalk while blood saturated her clothes and began to puddle on the broken cement.

That's me, thought Jersey. That puddle is me.

CITY HOSPITAL
6:00 P.M.

Seth hated having to learn things.

He liked knowing everything already.

The worst possible scene was being a jerk in front of people. Strangers (or far worse, friends) would find out that you didn't know what you were doing.

So he was volunteering in the Emergency Room in order to learn everything before medical school. He would get relaxed with blood and gore, pain and violence. When at last he became a medical student, he would have the edge on every other future doctor.

What maddened Seth was that no matter how much they learned, volunteers continued to be totally ignorant.

Oh, sure, you knew which set of elevators to use when you wheeled a patient to CAT scan. Which corridor to the cafeteria. Which door to Medical Records.

But basically, being a volunteer was a terrific way to find out that you knew nothing, nobody was going to teach you anything, and no matter how helpful you were, you were in the way.

This was a famous teaching hospital, and when they brought a gunshot wound into Trauma, supposedly you could go in and watch them explore the wound, administer the anesthesia, remove the bullet, and sew it up. But in fact, the room was so full of doctors, residents, nurses, techs, and police that somebody was bound to sweep you back into the hallway like a disposable glove that had fallen to the floor. When they hooked up a cardiac arrest to a monitor, supposedly you could learn what they were doing. But in fact, the tech accomplished the event so fast, and moved on to the next one so fast, that you never quite saw what was going on. And while Seth had not really expected that when they gave a patient a shot in the buttocks, he would get to practice, still he had not expected the nurse to draw the curtains shut and tell him to come back later.

Once Seth coaxed an aide to show him how to set up a sterile tray for suturing a minor wound. (Seth always learned a task the first time around; that was his rule. Learning it the first time spared him the trouble of going back and studying.) So once he saw how the sterile tray was done, he knew he would always be able to do it himself without errors.

But did the tech let Seth prepare the next sterile tray? No. In fact, the tech was pretty exasperated. "Look, this is my job," said the technician. "You're a volunteer. You run errands. I went to school for this stuff, buddy. Just because I spent five minutes with you, you still don't know from nothing."

Every year of his life, Seth had waited for adulthood.

When he was eleven, he had finally been old enough for his own paper route But it didn't make him a grown-up; it just made him get up at dawn and deliver twenty-four papers.

When he was thirteen and started seventh grade he expected to be a grown-up. No. He was just taller and gawkier.

Okay, when he was sixteen, and had a driver's license, then he'd be able to do everything. No. All he could do was errands for his mother — pick up a quart of milk or take his sister to the orthodontist.

Fine. When he was eighteen, he'd be a grown-up; he'd go to college, vote, have a girlfriend, and be unsupervised.

Well, here he was, eighteen, at college, unsupervised, and what was he doing? Running errands.

When was this kid stuff coming to a halt? When did he actually get to be a grown-up?

Speaking of girls — although not, regretably, girlfriends — he spotted Diana Dervane down the hall, on her way to check in. Her hair, shorter than his, was black and crisp and incredibly cute. Her cheeks were unevenly ruddy pink, as if she had just been working out. Diana always wore earrings so unusual he wanted to lean forward and study them. Then his thoughts would begin to spiral downward from her ears — throat, shoulder, breast . . .

"Volunteer," said a passing nurse. She did not really look at Seth because he was merely a volunteer and she was not required to make eye contact with lowlifes. "Blood Lab," she said, handing him a plastic bag labelled BIO-CHEMICAL HAZARD. Inside, a tube of blood awaited analysis.

Seth yanked a size large pair of disposable gloves from one of the boxes lining the countertops and jerked them over his hands. The talcum powder with which they were lined sifted softly between his fingers. The first time he'd put these on, he'd had doctor fantasies so bad he almost took over the Trauma Room.

Seth managed to laugh at himself (not one of his strong suits) and took the plastic bag. He read the physician's instructions on the form, but didn't know the abbreviations. Trying to be casual and surprised, he glanced up when Diana was only a few steps away.

He was crazy about her, and last week had gotten up his courage to ask her out — furious with himself that it took courage and more furious that he had had to rehearse the question. Diana had said yes to the date, but she sure hadn't said yes to anything else.

The evening was a disaster. Diana spent the whole time telling him how much he annoyed her.

It turned out that everything about Seth annoyed her. He even stood in the hall, Diana said, in an arrogant fashion. He spoke to the patients as if he were their doctor, not the volunteer pushing their stretcher to X-ray. He talked as if he were prescribing the medicine, not running to the pharmacy to get it.

He supposed that she had it right, especially the part about standing like a doctor. The medical students were nervous and hunched, listening hard for every crumb of knowledge. The residents were tired and hostile, working so hard they didn't even have posture. But the doctors — the Attending Physicians who supervised the residents, the on-call specialists who arrived constantly, and the private doctors coming in for their own patients — they had a special walk.

Whether they were women or men, WASP, Jew, Chinese, Pakistani, Indian, or African, tall or short, plump or skinny, they were so very visibly *doctors*.

They possessed knowledge. They understood, they decided, they acted.

They knew.

Oh, how Seth wanted to know!

Diana met his eyes expressionlessly.

Seth plastered on his wide protective grin. In high school he had of course been voted Most Likely to Succeed, but he had also won Best Smile. He protected himself further by using the fewest possible out-loud syllables. He even skipped "hi" and said only, "Diana," with a slight nod to accompany it. He felt slightly sick chatting with somebody who not only saw through him, but disliked what she saw.

Diana actually stopped and beamed up at him. If only he could analyze smiles the way he could analyze chemicals! Was hers, too, pasted on? Hiding affection? Hiding loathing? Had their difficult date been so meaningless to her she'd forgotten it, and this was just a courtesy, this smile that was making his heart leap?

He couldn't help himself. His smile turned real just looking at her. She was so pretty. He loved being taller than Diana was. Okay, so it was sexist. The fact was that he felt more masculine, stronger and tougher, because she was little and he was big.

"So, Seth," she said with a smirk, pointing at his gloved hands. "Playing doctor again tonight?"

Well, okay, at least he knew Diana's smile was hiding contempt.

He managed to keep his own smile bright, although under the gloves his hands turned sweaty and it took a conscious effort not to clench them. He held up BIOCHEMICAL HAZARD. "Just taking the usual precautions."

But she was already ignoring him, saying hello to the clerk to get her own assignments for the evening.

Where did she get this power to ruin his night? He could control his grades, his roommate, his parents. . . . Why couldn't he control his emotions toward Diana Dervane?

Possibly because a girl like Diana could be put into a sickly pink volunteer jacket that hung wrong, was missing buttons, and had sagging pockets, and still be gorgeous.

Stop thinking gorgeous, he told himself. Instead think about changing nights. Come Tuesday instead of Monday. Then you don't have to work with her. Think about what a pain in the neck she is.

Neck visions, however, brought Seth's thoughts once more on a downward spiral.

CITY HOSPITAL
6:00 P.M.

The blotchy pink volunteer jackets were so hideous that Diana could only assume the color prevented people from stealing them. It was absolutely impossible to wear anything that would look decent with that shade. Even a plain white turtleneck looked awful, her small head sticking up out of the pink and white as if she really did have the neck of a turtle.

She attached her photo ID and hiked down long confusing corridors to the Emergency Room. Large when it was built, the hospital had acquired five major additions, connected by ells, above-the-road glass hallways, and underground tunnels. Diana loved thinking about everything that was happening here — every operation, every tragedy, every lab procedure, and every triumph. Most of all she loved knowing that one day she would be a medical student here.

Okay, so she was only a college freshman now. Just wait. She'd train at this very hospital and have the edge on everybody.

The ER was built like a letter H, with four treatment halls jutting off the control area: surgical, medical, psychiatric, and pediatric. Special rooms were set aside for eye injuries, broken bones, and police holding. Next to the ambulance arrival pad was the real excitement: the Trauma Room, where the most badly injured patients were rushed.

Rush was the right word. It gave Diana a rush just to be here. Adrenalin spurted, making her hot and eager to see everything there was to see.

Of course, the instant she had to check in with the clerk, she would come down off the high. Meggie detested volunteers, especially college volunteers. They were just annoying do-gooders who got lost making pharmacy runs, and had to have their hands held when things got rough.

Diana turned down the final hall to see Seth standing between her and the desk clerk.

Wonderful. The humiliation of their only date made her cheeks burn and her temperature rise.

Seth was a hunk. Hair as black as her own, but longer, thicker, more casual. Eyes that burned blue, like some alien fire. Whenever their paths crossed, Diana found herself studying Seth inch by inch, starting at eye level, which for her, on Seth, was midchest. Seth was very buttoned up, and she imagined unbuttoning him.

If only he weren't so arrogant! You couldn't even apply to their college unless you were pretty full of yourself, but when it came to ego, you could stack Seth's next to anybody's. Seth was only a college freshman, but he already considered himself a medical student, a doctor, a Nobel Prize winner, and God.

Diana never talked to Seth without wanting to put him down.

Sure enough, she accomplished it first sentence out, which pleased her, and she moved right along to the desk clerk. "Here I am, Meggie," said Diana cheerfully. "How are you tonight?"

Poor choice of question. Meggie was never well. Her feet hurt, her head ached, and her fillings fell out. She liked to take these problems out on healthy people, like, for example, this perky, bouncy little rich girl with the glowing cheeks.

Meggie actually smiled, which meant she had something unpleasant to assign. "Insurance," said Meggie gloatingly, "needs a volunteer."

Diana stared at Meggie. *"Insurance?* No way! Stuck filling out insurance forms?"

Who do you think I am? (She just barely

kept herself from saying that out loud.) *I don't go to just any college, you know!*

Meggie heard every word even if Diana didn't say anything. She smirked.

Seth's grin remained in place like a computer spreadsheet.

Perfect for his personality, she thought.

"What's *my* assignment, Meggie?" he said.

Seth looked terrific even in a salmon-pink jacket that didn't fit. Possibly why Meggie was shipping Diana off to Insurance. The better to flirt with Seth. Well, Meggie could have him.

Meggie did not smile, which meant she had good news for Seth. "After you get back from the Blood Lab, Trauma needs a runner."

Sexist! thought Diana, absolutely furious at Meggie. You're giving him the good stuff because he's cute and male. "I don't want to do Insurance," she said. I volunteered to help save the world, she thought, not help insure it.

Meggie shrugged. "I got no work for you down here." Her enormous bosom strained against the shiny lime-green blouse she wore every Monday. Why couldn't the woman expand her wardrobe? She certainly had no trouble expanding her waist.

Seth was laughing at Diana. "Hey, have fun," he said. "Fill out an insurance form for me, huh?"

"How about I just lose you in the computer?" Diana stomped away, even though she was afraid. To reach Insurance, you had to go through the Waiting Room, a frightening hostile place Diana preferred to avoid.

Inner-city patients were okay when they were confined to stretchers and surrounded by techs and nurses and doctors, stuck with needles and fastened to machines. They weren't people then, really, but patients, which was something else altogether. Their ages and races, criminal backgrounds or tragedy or confusion blended into the bedsheets and the ward activity. They were so much cleaner, somehow, in the treatment area. Out in the Waiting Room, however, you actually had to be among them; and out there, they were not yet patients.

Sullen, frightened, pain-ridden people sat tensely in turquoise plastic chairs bolted to the floor. Some would wait ten minutes to be seen and some would wait hours. They suffered every possible woe and wound, and had nothing to do in that Waiting Room but get angry that they had to wait.

Sick mothers had no baby-sitters and had to bring their small children; a gunfight over a drug sale brought in the families of both the shooter and the shot; babies screamed and children whined and people missed meals and work and appointments.

Diana passed through a sea of hostile black, Asian, Indian, Hispanic, and white faces. Again tonight there was a yawning policeman sitting next to a man in shackles. The room was so packed that Diana could not make a detour, but had to step over the man's stretched-out legs. He smelled.

She reached Insurance alive, however, and tried to calm herself.

"A volunteer!" said a sexy black woman from behind a glass wall. She had fabulous fingernails and intricate hair. "Great. We're swamped." She actually smiled at Diana.

Diana had learned that her name tag meant nothing. Nobody would ever call her Diana. They would just shout, "Volunteer! Pharmacy!" In spite of past experience, though, Diana attempted conversation. "I'm always surprised that Mondays are so busy," she confided. "I thought Friday or Saturday would be the night the ER gets swamped."

"Nope. Nobody wants to ruin their weekend. People try to stay well or not think about it during the weekend. Monday it hits the fan." Knika handed her a form covered with a nurse's scribbles. "I'm Knika, Diana. You'll help us get paper. We chase after every patient, or else find their family, and get the facts for the computer."

Diana felt marginally better. She would at least know how everybody got hurt.

Knika listed the facts Diana would unearth. "Name, address, phone number, next of kin, and insurance or welfare status."

Immediately Diana felt worse again. She could not care less about anybody's insurance status. At this very moment, Seth was probably assisting on ⬩ GSW. (Actually neither Diana nor Seth had ever seen a gunshot wound, but they kept hoping.) "Do they have to have insurance to be treated?" she asked.

"Nope. This is City Hospital, honey. Everybody gets treated here, which is why it's so crowded. If they don't have insurance and they don't have welfare either, write down 'self-pay,' even if you know perfectly well that nobody is ever going to pay the bill."

WILLIAMS, said the sheet which Knika thrust at her. MALE. ETOH. FISTFIGHT. BROKEN NOSE. URGENT.

Knika picked up the phone, having finished with Diana.

This was not what Diana considered extensive job training and she had no idea what to do next. Diana took her paper to the Admitting Nurse, whose name tag said BARBIE. Diana could not imagine anybody who less resembled a Barbie doll. Nor could she imagine a Ken ever setting foot in this Waiting Room to meet her. "What do I do next?" she said to Barbie.

Barbie was incredulous. A volunteer dared talk to her? "I'm busy," she said sharply. (Another Seth.)

"I'll do the first one with you," said an

insurance clerk, popping out of her cubicle. She was barely five feet tall, slender, blonde, middle-aged. "I'm Mary. It seems a little zoo-y, doesn't it? That's because it is. It's Monday. Mondays are zoos."

In spite of the fact that everybody including children in the Waiting Room was bigger than Mary, Mary strode through the place as if it were empty. Diana felt brave enough to inspect the room. She actually focussed her eyes. Yes. Everybody there qualified for zoo status. In fact, she would have felt a lot better about one man in the corner if he were in a cage.

"*Urgent* means they took him straight to treatment," Mary said, decoding the scribbles on Diana's work sheet, "so you won't find him in the Waiting Room. These numbers here are the ambulance code. They tell you what part of town Mr. Williams was brought from. The *W* means he's white. That'll help us find him; we won't be looking for anybody black or Hispanic."

Help us find him? thought Diana. There weren't really rooms in the ER — just numbered, curtained partitions — but how could a patient be lost and have to be found?

Mary kept on. "This little check mark tells you the police are involved. So you don't want to assume you're safe around Mr. Williams. Make sure he's restrained."

Diana was not too sure she wanted to associate with somebody who might not be safe and needed to be restrained.

"There's only a last name," Mary said, "so probably he's too drunk to remember his first name."

"How do you know he's drunk?"

"That's what ETOH means. I forget what that stands for. Alcohol, I guess."

Down in the treatment area, a washable wall chart was Magic Markered with patients' last names and room numbers. WILLIAMS had no number, only the letter *H*. "Hall," explained Mary. "Drunks just get lined up because we have so many. Look for a broken nose."

The inner wall running down the Medical to Surgical wing was lined with stretchers, onto which men were fastened with leather bracelets, ankle grips, or twisted ropes made of bedsheets. Diana usually clung to the opposite wall when she walked here, because these patients were prone to smelling, swearing, and spitting. She had never run an errand involving the hall patients and could not imagine actually having to talk to one of them.

In the ER, patients were either "attractive" or "not attractive." It was easier for the staff to be sympathetic to a clean, well-spoken person who'd had an unfortunate accident than to a filthy stinking drunk who got scraped off the sidewalk week in and week out. The people lining these halls were very thoroughly "not attractive."

Diana did not think she knew how to look for a broken nose, but when they found Mr. Williams, she did. His nose had been crushed right back into his face. Blood had dried all over his shirt and turned the sheets red around his head. He looked dead to Diana, who wanted to cry.

Mary displayed no interest in Mr. Williams's possible pain. "Mr. Williams!" she yelled, grabbing his arm and shaking him.

Mr. Williams's eyes opened. "Whuh."

"What's your first name, Mr. Williams?"

"Whuh."

"Where do you live, Mr. Williams?"

"Whuh."

"Mr. Williams!" yelled Mary. "Answer me! What's your first name?"

"André."

Diana filled in "André."

"Now ask him where he lives," Mary told her.

"Where do you live, Mr. Williams?" asked Diana politely.

Two doctors and a nurse walking by laughed at her. She blushed and felt stupid.

"Yell," Mary told her.

Of course Seth had to choose this moment to reappear. He leaned against the far wall, arms crossed in a leisurely superior fashion, laughing at her for the second time in ten minutes. This isn't fair! thought Diana, cheeks scarlet with confusion and embarrassment. I didn't volunteer so I could get street addresses from drunks! "Where do you live, Mr. Williams?" she said again, and got no response. Finally she really yelled. *"Where do you live, Mr. Williams?"*

Mr. Williams told her where to go.

Diana turned pale.

The nurse who had laughed came back, grabbed Mr. Williams's arm, and shouted, "You tell her where you live or I'll leave you strapped to this stretcher for the next ten years, buddy!"

Mr. Williams grinned beneath his crushed nose. To Diana's surprise it was a friendly grin, and she found herself grinning back at him. "Texas," he said.

"Oh, right," said the nurse sarcastically. "What are you doing two thousand miles away then?"

"Giving you a hard time."

Everybody laughed, even Diana. Mr. Williams told her where he really lived (three blocks away) and to Diana's surprise, he said, "Hey, honey, I didn't mean to scare you. I had one too many."

"You had ten too many," said the nurse. "Who hit you, anyway?"

"My girlfriend's boyfriend," said Mr. Williams. He winked at Diana. Diana thought it sounded like the sort of situation where you would get a broken nose even if you hadn't had ten too many.

On the way back to Insurance, Diana said to Mary, "Why didn't we just let him sleep? Why did we put him through that? Shaking him and yelling at him?"

"We have to know which Mr. Williams this is," said Mary. "Say we've treated fifty men named Williams this year. Say we're guessing this guy is a drunk with a facial injury. But say what we don't know is, he's actually diabetic. He could die from the wrong treatment. So we want the right Patient Record for the doctors to look at before they prescribe. Plus, it's nice if the Mr. Williams who is actually here is the Mr. Williams who gets billed for being here."

At Knika's desk, Mary grabbed another form and handed it to Diana. "I'll put Mr. Williams in the computer," said Mary, "while you do the next one. Don't screw up."

Mary vanished into her cubicle.

Knika talked fiercely into her telephones.

Barbie helped a limping old man into a wheelchair.

Two minutes of training. That was it. A world-famous, world-class hospital, where if Diana got the wrong information, some innocent patient would die.

THE CITY
6:05 P.M.

Anna Maria refused to cry. She was too old for that and anyway, she had been in charge plenty of times without tears.

It was just that without electricity, the tiny apartment was so scary.

The lights wouldn't go on, the television wouldn't work, the radio didn't play. The stove didn't heat and the refrigerator didn't keep things cold.

It was hard not to cry. Tears filled her up, not behind the eyes, where they belonged, but inside her chest, making a well of hot water that threatened to drown her.

The streets were dangerous at night. It was not safe to be out there. Night began early in the City. As the sun lowered in the sky, it was hidden quickly by tall buildings. Long shadows darkened the little apartment. Anna Maria wanted to go outside so much it was a cry from her heart. Outside there would be people and talk and laughter.

Usually, nights, they got that from TV and radio. But not without electricity. Mama said it was her fault they didn't have electricity, because Mama hadn't paid the bill. She said in winter they didn't cut you off, but in summer they did.

Anna Maria felt so very cut off. As if huge cruel scissors had taken away all sound and light and hope.

The walls closed in and the heat was suffocating.

It was still light out and the quiz shows with their laughing emcees, or the reruns with their familiar leads, would be on now if she had a television. But she didn't. The hours stretched ahead of Anna Maria, black and silent and scary.

She did not know when Mama would be home. Mama never said. So they had Froot Loops for supper.

Anna Maria fixed Yasmin's hair, braiding it carefully. Then she filled a baby bottle with red Kool-Aid and stuck José into the stroller, his little hands wrapped around his bottle. Together she and Yasmin bumped the stroller down four flights of stinking, narrow, unlit stairs.

The sidewalk was bumpy and Anna Maria kept having to tilt the stroller to keep the wheels going. Yasmin danced the whole way. Yasmin had new shoes from the Salvation Army store and the heels were hard. She had never had hard-soled shoes before, only sneakers, and she loved the taps that the new shoes could make. Yasmin wanted to dance more than anything. A few blocks from their apartment was a dancing school, and Yasmin liked to pretend she went there.

José sucked on the bottle without tipping the Kool-Aid into his mouth. He would save the liquid for later; now he just wanted the comfort of the nipple in his mouth.

They walked quite a few blocks. Nothing happened to them. This was partly because Anna Maria was holding very tightly to the gold cross on her necklace, and partly because it was too early for people to be really drunk or really high or really dangerous.

It wasn't even dark enough for the streetlights to come on yet. Anna Maria hated streetlights. Most of them didn't work anyway, and the ones that did cast a sick pool of yellow that turned the faces of strangers into vampires.

Last year they had spent a lot of evenings at the public library because the children's room was friendly. But the library had run out of money, too. Anna Maria thought of the books in there, silent and closed like the doors. You never thought a library could close.

If a library could close, maybe even a hospital could close.

Anna Maria shivered.

The flimsy stroller caught on a crack in the sidewalk, and she was horrified for a moment that a wheel had broken. How could they replace the stroller? Yasmin knelt beside the wheel, extricated it, and got it started again. Anna Maria drew a breath of relief.

Just ahead was the neon sign she wanted:

EMERGENCY ROOM

She had been here plenty of times. Never on her own, though. But she knew several things about the Waiting Room at City Hospital.

It was air-conditioned.
It had a working television on the wall.
It was full of people and noise and things to
    watch.
There was a water fountain to drink from.
They gave you crayons and paper while you
    waited.

Anna Maria paused briefly where the sidewalk curved beneath huge pillars. People were lined against the walls smoking cigarettes because you weren't allowed to smoke inside a hospital. Two cars pulled up, and people got out and walked into the ER. Either they weren't too sick to walk, or else they were visiting other people who were. Then the drivers drove on to the parking lot. A security guard came out, his hand resting lightly on the butt of his gun while his radio, on the other hip, shouted with static.

Anna Maria took Yasmin's hand and pushed the stroller forward. Big silent glass doors opened automatically when their combined weight triggered the controls.

On the other side of the doors she quickly assessed the situation. The Admitting Nurse was taking somebody's pulse. The desk secretary was answering phones. The inside security guard was yelling at a drunk.

Anna Maria slid past a man in a wheelchair, two fat women reading old magazines, and a pregnant woman with tears rolling down her cheeks.

Anna Maria sat down in one of the plastic seats and pulled the stroller in close. Yasmin hung onto the stroller handle and looked around. José sucked on his bottle.

Oh, it was so nice in here! The air was cool and comfortable. The fat women looked friendly. Somebody had abandoned a bag of potato chips on the coloring table. Anna Maria would wait a little bit and if nobody came, she would share the chips with her brother and sister.

The TV was showing the news.

Anna Maria would not have chosen the news herself, but she loved being talked to, and the man on Channel 8 was talking in that warm, solid, comforting way.

Nobody noticed the children.

They were safe. They could stay hours, as long as José was good.

José was two.

Yasmin was four.

Anna Maria was eight.

THE WAITING ROOM
6:17 P.M.

Diana prayed there were family members in the Waiting Room to give her the necessary statistics. She stood on the rim of the packed room, as nervous as a bungee jumper on the edge of his bridge. "Sczevyl?" she whispered. Funny-looking name. What if it was spelled wrong, or she was saying it wrong? It didn't matter, nobody so much as glanced at her. Whispering in the Waiting Room was clearly ridiculous. She, who hated to raise her voice and be obvious, had to shout. "Sczevyl!" she yelled, pronouncing it "shovel."

If there were family members in the Waiting Room, they didn't pronounce it shovel. Therefore, she had to find the patient.

Diana went back to Mary, hoping for help on her second work sheet as well. "What exactly does this mean — urgent, female, psychotic, abusive, swearing?"

Mary surveyed the sheet. "Offhand, using medical terminology, I'd say the woman's nuts."

Diana tried to laugh.

"It means she was fighting," explained Mary. "Fighting probably means kicking, screaming, biting, hitting. That kind of stuff. See the check in this box? Police are involved."

"Neat."

Mary laughed. "She'll be in CIU. Crisis Intervention Unit. That's supposed to sound less threatening than calling it Psychiatric. The door's that big thick slab of glass at the end of Hall Four. It's locked. You have to knock. Guards let you in and let you out. Don't be scared."

Don't be scared.

Right.

Diana actually squared her shoulders to walk down the hall to CIU. Her hands were sweating and her knees hurt. She wanted to be a doctor, but she wanted her patients to be clean, neat people who talked normally.

Crisis Intervention Unit? What kinds of crises were they intervening in? And did she, Diana, wish to intervene?

What if she intervened when a fist or a foot was lashing out? Not to mention a gun or a knife?

Seth fell into step with her. "So how's Insurance?"

Diana was sorry that Seth was so attractive. His looks kept provoking her interest. She wrenched her thoughts and eyes away from Seth's buttons. "It's pretty interesting. I haven't actually done any insurance. What have you been doing?"

"MVAs and GSWs," said Seth casually. Motor vehicle accidents and gunshot wounds.

Diana put him down instantly. She had time to stop herself but didn't. "You mean they admitted an MVA and a GSW. I asked what *you* did."

Seth put on his usual big sprawling Texas-sized grin. "Nothing," he admitted. "They kicked me out of Trauma. I hardly got to see a thing."

"Did you see the gunshot wound itself though?" whispered Diana. She didn't want anybody to overhear; how perverted she would sound, hungering after the sight of a GSW. What did it really look like? A round hole? No chest where once a chest had been?

"No, but if I do, I'll give you details," Seth promised.

Diana was not grateful. She liked to be the one who knew everything first, not the one who found out secondhand. She struggled with jealousy. I'm investing too much emotion into a simple volunteer night at a hospital, she thought. The thing is, I want to be a doctor, and working in Insurance isn't fair.

"Want to go to Blood Lab with me?" said Seth. "We can stop at the vending machine room on the way and get a Coke."

Diana raised her eyebrows. "I'm in a hurry, Seth," she said, to let him know he didn't understand hurrying. Nothing he did mattered. "This is important."

"Oh," said Seth, hanging onto his relentless grin. "Where are you headed?"

"Psychotic admission." Diana shrugged as if she'd done this plenty of times. *What is it with me and cute guys?* she thought. *I go out of my way to make sure they know that just because they're cute doesn't mean they can get anything past me.*

But why would I want an adorable hunk like Seth to get past me?

There was not, however, time for an in-depth analysis of her feelings toward men. She was already striding up to the locked bullet-proof door of the Crisis Intervention Unit.

Was Seth impressed by how calmly she knocked? She would never know. Once inside, she was too scared to look back.

The attendants, clad in operating room outfits, like pea-green pajamas, were large enough to frighten football tackles. Who was scarier? The patients or the immense men in charge?

An elderly, silent male patient in need of a shave sat on a disheveled stretcher. He was staring at nothing but talking to it anyway

Desperate, filled-with-dread cries poured from his mouth. Somehow Diana knew it was not a foreign language. Just helpless, hopeless pleading. With nobody.

A middle-aged woman had been sobbing for hours. Red-eyed, patchy-faced, and exhausted from tears, she glanced at Diana and turned away, bursting into tears yet again.

A girl Diana's own age was fastened down on her stretcher by the same thick leather anklets and bracelets that locked the drunks to theirs. A twisted sheet locked up and over her shoulders, flattening her out on the stretcher. Beneath the wrist locks were thick bandages, and another bandage covered her throat.

Diana could not bear to think what this girl had done to herself.

The largest attendant lounged around, while she surveyed his selection of patients. This was not a man with whom Diana would ever choose to argue. MAURICE, said his name tag. It was the kind of name you got teased for, but she would bet her inheritance nobody ever teased this Maurice. "Who you want?" said Maurice, chewing gum between words.

Diana did not want any of these patients.

She certainly did not want to talk to any of them about their insurance status. How could the hospital make her bother people in such despair? Was she supposed to grab this sobbing woman or this manic man and demand their phone numbers?

I hate this! she thought. "Sczevyl?" she said.

Maurice pointed to the girl.

This was the fighting, kicking, screaming, swearing psychotic? Diana gulped. "Miss Sczevyl? I need to ask a few questions."

The girl did not move. She did not change the focus of her eyes nor acknowledge that she had heard.

"Would you tell me your next of kin, please?" said Diana.

No response. It would have been less frightening if the girl had screamed and sworn. The deadlike person lying there was impossible to look at.

"We'd like to know who she is, too," Maurice said. "We want to let the kid's family know what's happening. So far she doesn't want to tell us anything."

The silence broke. "I told you to leave me alone!" screamed the girl, her voice huge, like trumpets. She tried to free herself, hurling herself up and down even though it was impossible to lunge at all. She fought so hard, the mattress began to inch out from under her. Her skull thwacked violently against the now-exposed metal of the stretcher.

Diana could readily believe this girl had enough strength to break leather bonds. She stepped back. I could be home listening to the radio, she thought.

"Come on, honey, that's not helping." Maurice yanked the mattress back up under the girl.

"I don't want to help! Let me out of here! I hate you! I didn't ask to come here! Let me go!"

The volume of her screaming was unbelievable. Yet, the other patients never so much as looked her way. They were caught in their own broken hearts.

"Ask away, honey," said Maurice. This time "honey" meant Diana.

On campus, it was not considered good form to call a woman honey or dear or sweetie. It was a putdown. In the ER, however, it was a quick way to show kindness and also, of course, to skip all that effort involved in reading name tags.

Diana could not remember when she had felt so inappropriate but she asked, "Would you tell me your street address, please?"

For the second time in ten minutes, somebody told Diana exactly, profanely, where to go. Miss Sczevyl meant it. She wanted Diana in hell. Perhaps that was where Miss Sczevyl was, and she needed company.

Abruptly, the girl's volume vanished. She stopped struggling and became motionless again. She was as silent and still as a corpse.

But rigid, as if her muscles had turned to wire.

"It'll be all right," comforted Diana. Why had she said that? What if Miss Sczevyl had the kind of life where it would not be all right?

Tears slid down the patient's cheeks to bury in her hair and dampen the sheets. The motionless face seemed not to be producing the tears, just lying beneath them.

Diana could not bear it that the girl was so alone. The girl needed her mother or her sister or her best friend. "I could call home for you," said Diana. "Or call somebody else. Who do you want me to call?"

"I want you to go away. You don't know me. I don't know you. I don't care what you do, and you don't care what I do."

Gee, I have a flair for this, thought Diana. I can dedicate my life to helping depressed people.

At least Diana was spared having to demand how the girl intended to pay for the privilege of being strapped to a stretcher. A person who wouldn't give her parents' names wasn't going to turn over her insurance card, either. "How do you know her name is Sczevyl?" she asked Maurice, thinking that she could look in the girl's purse for addresses.

"We don't. She was wearing a jacket with that name written inside on the collar tag.

Jacket could be stolen or borrowed or bought used."

"Is your name Sczevyl?" Diana asked.

The patient said nothing.

There was nothing on her face.

There was nothing in her eyes.

She seemed to have stepped out of her body.

Gone wherever she meant to go in spite of being strapped to the mattress.

Diana shuddered convulsively.

Maurice did not. That a patient's personality could exit from the body without death was all in an evening's work to him.

Diana walked back to Mary. I learned one thing tonight, she thought. I'm not likely to become an Emergency Room psychiatrist.

Mary entered the patient as Unknown.

And she is, thought Diana. Nobody knows her name, her heart, or her despair, and that's how she wants it.

To be completely unknown. Surely the ultimate horror.

It was a thought that required talk, and the only person Diana knew well enough for talk was Seth. She would forgive him for his past sins and his present arrogance and go for a Coke after all. They would discuss Unknowns. It was the sort of philosophic topic that college freshmen could kick around for days.

She found Seth among the medical students who were giving reports. Seth had taken off his volunteer jacket and was standing in his white button-down collar shirt and dark tie, arms folded casually across his broad chest, back propped against the wall.

He was pretending to be a medical student.

Volunteers were known exclusively by their salmon-pink jackets. He didn't have one. Nobody would recognize him as the college kid who volunteered Mondays.

And the medical school was so big, the students probably didn't know each other any more than Diana knew everybody on the undergraduate campus.

If the Attending asked Seth a question, which Seth certainly could not answer, and he was caught, what would happen to him?

But what if he weren't caught? If Seth were assigned an actual task — like drawing blood — would he really dare try it?

To Seth's left was a tiny Chinese woman, who could not weigh a hundred pounds, and whose black hair was as thick and long as a draft horse's tail. To his right was a weedy, stooped young man with lopsided glasses, a cartoon of the nerdy scientist. Behind the nerd stood a handsome wide-jawed blond man, central casting's television doctor. Next to the blond was a young woman who was wonderfully pretty. Somebody you could be best friends with, somebody who laughed a lot.

Somebody, thought Diana with a surprising

twitch of jealousy, that Seth could have a crush on.

The medical students shifted in order to study a document the Attending held. Sure enough, Seth moved next to the very pretty girl, and they smiled at each other.

"Volunteer!" shouted Meggie, waving a pharmacy sheet.

Seth didn't move. Miss Pretty Medical Student was busy borrowing a pencil from Seth's shirt pocket. She was having much more fun extricating the pencil than listening to the Attending. Seth likewise. Their eyes met and his black shock of hair moved a little closer to her long gleaming brown hair. Seth's computerized smile began spreading.

I hope you get caught, thought Diana, taking the drug order only because pharmacy runs were better than asking psychotic women for their phone numbers. I hope Miss Pretty Medical Student asks to see your ID. I hope the Attending asks you to draw blood and they arrest you for assault when you try it.

Seth looked up and Diana curled her lip at him.

He just grinned and mimed a passionate kiss. Diana remembered the real kiss the night of the difficult date, and thought — Why wasn't I nice?

Both Meggie and Miss Pretty Medical Student blew Seth a kiss back.

EMERGENCY ROOM
6:23 P.M.

They were sewing up the hand of a boy who had ripped his palm open on the broken glass of a car window. He'd probably been trying to take the stereo out, but nobody commented on this. The students crowded eagerly around the bed on which the boy sat, feet dangling, pale and shivering with fear. Nobody likes the thought of needles stitching in and out of their very own personal flesh.

The pretty brunette was regarding Seth with cheerful, but slightly speculative eyes. Either she wanted to flirt more intensively, or she wanted to check his photo ID.

If they catch me, it'd go on my record, he thought. Nobody at this hospital would laugh. Responsible future doctors don't masquerade. Pretending to be a medical student could stop me from being accepted at medical school.

I'm not chicken, he told himself quickly. I'm sensible.

He wondered if girls — particularly girls named Diana — thought sensible was more interesting than daring. He managed to drift away as the real students trooped after the Attending. There was confusion in the eyes of the pretty doctor. She was wondering why Seth wasn't standing next to her.

I could have gotten away with it, he thought.

But there was not enough room around the bed for Seth to join them. He leaned against the wall just beyond the curtain, alternately chewing himself out for not being an imposter and congratulating himself for having enough brains to back out now.

He listened to a clear but shaky narration, the voice of a very nervous student addressing a patient for the first time. "Now, I'm going to — ummm — give you a shot first, to kill the pain, and I'm — um — going to do this — um — very slowly — and — um — you tell me — um — if it hurts."

A nurse near Seth was laughing. "The old, I'm-going-to-do-this-very-slowly trick."

"Trick?"

"When you've never done something before in your life, you have to do it slowly," said the nurse. "But now the patient thinks the wonderful doctor is doing it slowly because he's kind and understanding." Her face changed.

"Hah. Show me the medical student who is kind and understanding. They're all pushy and grasping."

It was what Diana had said. He didn't want to be pushy and grasping, but he wanted to be a doctor, and sweet slow-moving types did not get into medical school. Reluctantly Seth took his volunteer jacket back from where he had tucked it, behind stacks of folded blankets.

He considered the air kisses. Forget Meggie. But the pretty medical student — truly hot. Probably around twenty-three or four. Seth imagined dating a woman four or five years older, with four or five years more experience. Forget medical experience. Think sexual experience. This was so rewarding, he stayed with the vision.

Diana's kiss was the one he wanted and he did not want it in the air. Maybe the air kisses made her jealous. He decided to see if Diana had had a change of heart and headed for the Admitting Nurse's desk. Insurance was back behind there and he could air kiss over the glass barriers and make Diana's heart race.

Right.

He loved to listen to Barbie question incoming patients. She was so cool. Nothing frazzled this woman. Seth wanted to be exactly like her, so no situation that walked up, was wheeled up, or got dragged in would make him bat an eye.

She was a large woman, and wore even larger scrubs, so she looked as big and green as a tank. She was chewing cinnamon gum, a habit Seth mostly observed in the ambulance crews. The aroma kept you from getting nauseous when you had to take a deep whiff of your own patient.

A youngish man sat in front of her complaining of severe chest pain. "What have you been taking?" asked Barbie, scrawling on the patient information sheet.

"Nothing," said the young man.

"Gimme a break," Barbie said irritably. "What were you drinking?"

The young man looked away.

Barbie chewed on her pen along with her gum. "My man, if you're having a heart attack or if your best friend stabbed you, how am I gonna know? You think I read minds? Talk to me or get out of the way, there are people in line behind you." She didn't even sound interested, and of course the worst thing when you get to an emergency room is if the nurse is not interested, so the man answered after all. "Vodka."

"How much?"

"Prob'ly — um — half a bottle."

"This your usual amount?"

"Yes."

"You eat anything today?"

"I had some lunch."

"What are you smoking?" said Barbie.

"Crack."

The nurse rolled up the man's sleeve to take his blood pressure. Tracks on the arm were visible. "What are you shooting?" she said.

"H."

She would not tighten the blood pressure cuff if he had just shot up, because the scab on the vein might burst. "What pills?" she said. "You swallow anything?"

Wow, thought Seth. The guy smokes crack, drinks vodka, does heroin, and takes pills. Talk about full-time activity. He wondered what Barbie saw, that he had not, knowing right away what was going on here.

"Nothing today. But — but — I think I OD'd," said the young man nervously. "I think I'm dying."

"You might be," agreed Barbie. "I mean, you poly-abuse like this, what do you think is gonna happen? You think your heart is just gonna shrug?"

Apparently the guy was in trouble, because Barbie didn't make him wait a single minute, but called an aide to wheel the addict back into Medical. She never glanced after him but turned to the patch from an ambulance that burst metallically from the speaker behind her desk. At the same time, three lines were ringing at Knika's desk. Seth listened greedily to everything.

"We are inbound to your facility with a two-seven female complaining of severe abdominal pain," shouted the patch. "Patient states she has had fever two days, currently at one oh three. Upon palpation abdomen is rigid in lower right quadrant. Patient currently receiving ten liters of oxygen and has line of normal saline. Blood pressure 140 over 100. Pulse 100. Respirations 30."

"Roger," said Barbie. She beckoned to the next patient slouching near her and began filling out two forms simultaneously: the new patient at her desk and the incoming. "What's your ETA?" she said to the ambulance.

"Fifteen minutes."

"Roger."

Seth murmured to Knika, "What's a two-seven?"

Knika gave him the sort of look Seth hated most. *You're in college and you can't deduce what a two-seven is?* "The patient, cupcake," said Knika, "is twenty-seven years old."

Cupcake? She dared called him cupcake? He who was going to go to medical school? He would never speak to Knika again. Or go near her desk. He walked away.

"You gonna say thank you, maybe, for the explanation?" said Knika.

Seth stopped, turned, took a deep breath, pasted a smile on his face and said, "Thank you, Knika."

"Hey, cupcake, any time."

Barbie hung up, laughing. "He gets into medical school, Knika, he's gonna snub you."

"Oh, no," said Knika. "I'm destroyed. Another white doctor snubbing me? Can I live through it?"

In his burning ears Seth heard Diana accusing him of becoming a doctor in order to have people admire him and treat him with awe. Telling him how pushy and arrogant he was.

He sat on the edge of Knika's desk. "When I go to the cafeteria, I'll bring you back a cookie." The hospital bakery made enormous, terrific chocolate chip cookies.

She laughed. "You gonna bribe your way out of this, cupcake?"

"Could you call me Seth instead of cupcake?"

"Nope. I never call teenagers by name. It gives them airs. They think they're worth something."

Routes 14-A and I-95
6:25 p.m.

"I can?" said Alec reverently.

"Sure." Alec's cousin punched him lightly. "Just don't hurt it. You would not believe what I paid for this baby."

The motorcycle was absolutely beautiful. Huge, heavy, gleaming, powerful — everything Alec had ever yearned for in a bike. And his cousin, decked out in leather — everything Alec had ever yearned for in clothes.

The girls were on the sidewalk, giggling. Alec didn't much like any of the three girls present, but they were still girls. Alec yearned for girls probably twice as much as for a motorcycle, which was a lot, and both seemed equally impossible to get.

He never understood girls' laughter. What were they laughing at?

He tried to believe they weren't laughing at him, they were just laughing, but whenever he looked their way, they dissolved again into giggles and he could not feel attractive, just stupid.

He had only been on a motorcycle twice before. This one was far heavier and more powerful.

His cousin was grinning.

Three girls were giggling.

The sun was hot and the pavement stretched out black and shimmering with heat waves.

Alec got on the bike. It was like a living creature beneath him. He could have taken its throbbing pulse. Its heart ached to accelerate, to leave a patch on the road. His new jeans were deep indigo blue against the glittering purple of the metallic paint job his cousin had special-ordered.

"Wear a helmet," said one of the girls.

Alec's cousin laughed. "You think he's a sissy or something?"

"You're supposed to wear a helmet," she said, her voice whiny and dictatorial, like a teacher nobody wanted to have.

Alec took off.

It was wonderful! The breeze he created became a wind, and his hair stood out behind him in a strangely sensual way. His fingers tightening around the controls felt longer and stronger, harder and more calloused. In a moment the girls and his cousin had vanished from sight, and then from his thoughts. There was nothing in Alec's mind but the feel of the motorcycle and the look of the road ahead.

He went a mile.

Two miles.

Took two minutes.

A third mile took less than a minute. The slightest crack in the road was like a ravine; he could feel its measure on the tires and between his legs.

Signs for the turnpike entrance appeared. INTERSTATE I-95 NORTH, LEFT OFF 14-A.

Alec knew his cousin did not have the turnpike in mind. His cousin expected him back about now. But if Alec went for a long drive, there was not a single thing his cousin could do about it. Of course, he'd never let Alec borrow the bike again. But so what? At least Alec could have the ride he'd wanted all his life.

Of course, he didn't want his cousin yelling at him in front of the girls. On the other hand, the girls would be impressed — if they were still there. Maybe Alec would drive for so long, the girls would have gone on home. What would his cousin do if he kept the bike for an hour? Or the whole evening?

When you sat on this huge vibrating monster, who cared?

Alec swung onto the entrance ramp and was instantly in trouble.

Maybe if he'd been in the middle of the ramp, or if he'd been going slower. But he made his decision a little late for such a hard right turn at such a high speed, and the back tire of the bike crested on a patch of sand and gravel.

Alec knew what was going to happen during the split second before it did.

What would his mother say? She was always after him to follow *precautions*. He hated that word. Not only were you supposed to be cautious, you were supposed to be cautious before that, too. *Pre*cautious.

Forget it. Real men took risks. That was what life was about.

There was enough time to realize that he had taken a lot more risk than he had meant to. Enough time to realize how fast he was going to hit the pavement. That he was wearing only a T-shirt and jeans. That he had just gotten his braces off a month ago and if he hit the road jaw first —

And then he was out of time.

THE CITY
6:30 P.M.

Response time was slower here in the City than out in the suburbs. They had more calls, more danger, more traffic. Three ambulances were required at the scene of the shooting. Although an ambulance could in fact carry two stretchers, especially in a gunfight, you didn't want to double up the victims.

One ambulance crew scraped up the college girl who had so foolishly walked into the middle of a drug dispute. "What are they thinking about, these university kids?" said the first cop on the scene, staring down at Jersey. "I mean, you'd think she'd notice."

"They're too full of themselves. Those snobby kids think they're God just 'cause they got into that school," said the driver.

"Or," said a second cop more gently, "they come from a place where it's actually safe to walk downtown. Poor kid. I'm glad I don't have to call her parents."

Jersey listened to and tried to analyze this conversation. Was she dying? Was this it? Her final moment on earth?

She wanted to be afraid, or at least to think about it, but she felt strangely floaty. Perhaps she was in the act of dying, her soul in the instant of drifting out of her body.

"Here's her name," said somebody. "Jersey MacAfee."

They must have found her purse then. She wondered if she still had the hundred dollars. She wondered how she could have been so eager to have yet another pair of black shoes.

"No, that's probably her address."

"No, it's her name."

A face leaned over her. It was in pieces, floating around like her soul — a nose here, a mouth there, eyes wandering in front of her. It was terrifying and she began to cry. Crying was a relief; it was a bodily function, so didn't that mean her body was still functioning? She wasn't dying yet?

"Jersey?" came a voice out of the floating features. "That's your name? Is that your name, honey?"

The cop could not believe the girl's name was Jersey. "Who would name their kid after a state?" he said irritably.

She wanted to tell them the romantic story behind it; her parents' honeymoon and her conception and the wonderful things that went along with her unusual name. But her mouth said, "Am I going to be all right? Am I going to die?" Oh, good! she thought. I can talk clearly. So things can't be that bad. It's just blood. They'll just pour a few pints in me and I'll be fine.

"We're going to do everything we can, honey," said the ambulance woman. She filled Jersey's mouth and throat with a plastic cylinder. Jersey panicked and tried to pull it out. Dimly she heard people telling her not to be afraid, but she was afraid, and kept fighting and then, horrifyingly, scarier by far than bullets and blood, she felt herself being tied down, as straps tightened across her chest.

THE WAITING ROOM
6:35 P.M.

Nobody cared that Diana was supposed to be doing Insurance. People stopped her continually. The ugly pink blotch of a jacket that she had to wear was a badge of safety and help.

She fixed an ice pack for a waiting patient whose knee was wrenched and received a teary thank you. She found a blanket for a woman who was shivering and a Spanish interpreter for a large family desperately worried about their uncle. From the Pediatric ER she borrowed a box of sad, stubby old crayons and some discarded computer paper for the two little girls at the children's table.

Armed guards sauntered around. They seemed only half there, as if they'd already had a long day and were now sleeping on their feet. Diana should have felt comforted by so much police presence, but instead she was more afraid. Why did the ER need so many? What kind of things happened out here in the Waiting Room anyhow?

She stood between Knika and Barbie, studying her latest form and trying to decide how to handle it. The med radio blared.

"Emergency Room, go ahead." Barbie continued filling out the form for the child with a sore throat while she listened to the med radio.

The patch was very loud. "Uh, yes, we're en route to your facility with three GSWs. A one-eight female . . ."

Diana swung around and stared at the telephone. Gunshot wounds? A one-eight female? I'm a one-eight female!

She listened to the recitation of blood pressure and pulse of a one-eight female, a one-four male, and a one-nine male.

Was this a street gang? Some horrible family shooting each other? Teenagers busily buying and selling drugs? Lunatics sniping off tall buildings?

Security promptly got on the PA system. "All visitors please report to the Waiting Room. No visitors may remain in the treatment areas. Until further notice, there will be no visiting of patients. Repeat. No visiting of patients by anybody."

The simmering rage in the Waiting Room picked up. Not only did this mean everybody had to wait even longer, but you couldn't go in with your relatives while they got treated. An old man who didn't speak English had his middle-aged daughter with him to interpret — tough. She stayed in the Waiting Room, he went in alone.

Guards ushered angry arguing family members and friends back to the Waiting Room. "We got gunshot wounds coming in," explained the guards. "Hospital rules. No visitors in back when we got gunshot wounds." They yanked gloves over their hands and waited for the ambulances.

Diana dropped her insurance sheet right back into the box. Let somebody else do it. She was not about to miss out on three GSWs.

TRAUMA ROOM
6:38 P.M.

There were so many revolving red lights that the ambulance bay looked like the Fourth of July.

The first ambulance backed up to the hospital doors and attendants lifted out the stretcher.

Triage teams were yanking on disposable gloves and over these, surgical gloves. Techs had finished tying clear plastic shoulder-to-floor aprons over the doctors' and nurses' clothes. The stretcher was so quickly surrounded by medical personnel that Diana could not see the patient, only the green cotton scrubs of the staff.

The second ambulance backed in.

In the moment before the patient was surrounded by the people who would try to save her life, Diana recognized her. *A girl from college.* She was in Diana's sociology lecture!

Diana cried out, unable to stop her horror

from surfacing. Nobody heard; there was too much racket. Sirens, police running in, police around the stretchers as much as doctors, walkie-talkies screaming staticky conversations, blood-gas technicians and specialists converging.

The patients were quickly slid off their ambulance stretchers and onto hospital beds. The ambulance attendants yanked their stretchers back out of the way and stood in the halls where they struggled with their own paperwork and made traffic impossible.

The sheets on which the girl had been lying were saturated with blood.

It was not possible. You did not attend college — certainly not *this* college — with the expectation of being shot on the street. You were there to study literature and philosophy and chemistry and find a boyfriend.

Diana could not remember the girl's name. It was something odd. Something she would not personally give a daughter of hers.

"Wait wait wait wait wait," said one of the cops to the Attending Surgeon. "You maybe got the shooter here in Bed Two, and his victims here in One and Three. Let's make real sure bed two here isn't still armed."

The surgeon thought that was a great idea and stepped back while the cops double-checked.

"It's always the way," said one resident to

another. "The shooters hardly even nick each other, they have such lousy aim, but they manage to get the bystander just fine."

Diana was close enough to see the resident cut the clothes off the nineteen-year-old. Supposedly he was the shooter, but if so he had also been shot. A gunshot wound, she saw now, was a hole. A black-looking thing with no spread to it. Not very threatening, really. Diana was amazed.

The victim was quite proud, looking down at his hole as if it were a prize in an Olympic festival. "This is my fourth," he said. "I been here three times already this year." How amazing, thought Diana. He can talk even with a hole in his chest. How come all the air isn't racing out of his lungs? How come he's not drenched with blood?

"How we gonna keep you alive, you keep behaving like this, kid?" said Steven, the male nurse.

The boy laughed. Keeping alive did not seem to be a priority with him.

"It isn't funny," said the doctor. "What about your mother? Your family? They happy that you live like this?"

"They probably on they way over," the boy said, laughing again. "Better than TV, you know."

Diana wanted to see everything. Her eyes

bounced back and forth, as if this were a tennis match, not an ER.

The team changed places, now rolling the girl onto her side, so they could work on both the entrance and the exit wound. They used the sheet to turn her, like a cloth spatula under a human pancake. They had cut away all her clothing. There was something dreadful about her nakedness, as if her body had become the lawful property of the trauma team.

The Attending frowned over the nineteen-year-old. "What's this wound on the back of your neck, kid?" The boys had refused to identify themselves, so they could not be called anything except "kid."

"I dunno."

The doctor prodded gently. "Kid. Is this a knife wound up here?"

"Could be."

"You got a knife wound *and* a gunshot wound? What kind of life you got here, kid?"

The boy smiled with satisfaction. "Exciting."

"And possibly over with!" snapped the Attending. "Roll the fourteen-year-old back into the hall," he said to Diana. "He's hardly scratched; we can get to him anytime."

Diana shoved the stretcher. Stretchers were much heavier than you expected them to be, and much harder to maneuver. They didn't like to roll in a straight line, but always aimed for

IV poles and visitors' legs. Panting, Diana got the stretcher into the hall and shoved it against a wall between two drunks.

Two cops took over. "Who shot you?" they said to the kid. They were writing in very tiny notebooks. Diana didn't have small enough handwriting to use anything that little. Maybe it was a special police skill. Writing in miniature.

"Huh? Who shot me?" said the fourteen-year-old. "I dunno. I din' see nothing."

"That guy in Bed Two shot you?"

"Huh? I dunno. I jest walkin' by."

"Kid, you got shot. You gotta tell us who did it."

"Can't. Din' see nothing."

"What was it about?"

"I dunno. I jest walkin' by."

"You dealing drugs?"

"What you mean? Me? I still in junior high."

"Yeah, and are you dealing?"

"Nah, man, I get straight A's. I be home studyin'." He couldn't keep a straight face during this and giggled softly to himself. He tested his bonds and smiled happily because he was indeed securely fastened.

Diana had absolutely no idea what on earth his thoughts might be.

Mary walked up, as uninterested in the GSWs as if she saw them every day of the week. But then, of course, she did. Diana tried to imagine such a thing, and remembered in some confusion that she herself hoped to be a surgeon and see this kind of thing every day of the week.

"Here," said Mary, "come on, we're swamped, do your share."

Diana took the sheet. How could life go on like this? Surely if there were three people shot, the rest of the world should slow down and give the hospital, and specially Diana, time to consider things. But the patients kept rolling in, and she kept having to find out their insurance status.

Trauma Room doors closed and Diana felt shut out of all excitement and all possibilities. The only good thing was that old Seth wasn't in there. He was probably off flirting with Miss Pretty Medical Student.

Diana made a face and stared down at her assignment. A man with SOB. In an Emergency Room, this trio of letters meant shortness of breath. Very serious. People who weren't getting enough air were people in danger of dying. They were never in the Waiting Room, always went straight to treatment.

She checked the wallboard for the patient's room number.

The name on the sheet registered in her mind. *Robert Searle.*

Her eyes glazed over. She could not think. Her mind went flat.

No, she said to herself. No, it's not the person I'm thinking of. Can't be. Impossible. I'm going home now. I'm out of here. I can't do this. She closed her eyes tightly, as if she could actually blot herself out of the ER.

Robert Searle. She would have to *look* at him. Talk to him. Hear his voice.

She remembered that she was eighteen and brilliant and she could handle things. She forced herself to open her eyes and look back down.

Robert Searle.

The name on the paper had not changed.

Only her life had changed.

ROUTES 14-A AND I-95
6:42 P.M.

Alec's own face was the brake that slowed him down.

He did not lose consciousness.

He knew exactly how long it took an ambulance to arrive.

Nobody tried to move him, and the two women who first stopped to help were not strong enough to get the motorcycle off his legs anyway.

The heat of the motorcycle exhaust pipe burned away his skin as he lay there. He could smell himself charring, even over the smell of gasoline and pavement and blood.

He wanted to scream but his mouth was full. He did not know how he was able to breathe. He was aware of more than he wanted to be: of how the elderly ladies were crying, of how somebody would have to notify his mother, of how his cousin was going to react about the bike. Did he have a face left? What was filling up his mouth and making it impossible to talk?

The siren was an oddly terrifying sound.

It sounded like arrest and rage, like police and prison.

He tried to think of it as his own rescue, but couldn't.

Along with the pain came a rush of fear so strong it was like the wind that had lifted his hair.

He could not move.

Was it the weight of the bike?

. . . or had he hurt his spinal cord?

THE WAITING ROOM
6:45 P.M.

Anna Maria was feeling secure.

Half an hour in the Waiting Room and she felt as if she knew everybody there. She was no longer afraid of them, and nobody had asked why she and José and Yasmin were sitting at the coloring table. Nobody ever would, either. As for the police, they were there to stop trouble, not start it.

For a few minutes a girl whose name tag read DIANA had sat at the low table and colored with them. Anna Maria loved that. Diana was so pretty and had such a nice pink jacket on. It made Anna Maria feel special to have Diana sit next to her. "Let's make get-well cards," Diana had said cheerfully. "Who is sick? Your mother? We'll make a card so she'll feel better."

Anna Maria smiled and pretended not to speak English.

Diana drew a garden of yellow flowers and

put a big red castle behind it, with orange towers and a blue dragon. Anna Maria and Yasmin were awestruck by this artwork and struggled to copy it. José leaned forward in his stroller to watch. Then he sucked on his bottle some more.

When Diana left to run an errand, Anna Maria carefully slipped the three best crayons into her pocket. When they got home, they would each have a crayon.

Behind Anna Maria sat perhaps a dozen patients waiting to be seen. With them were family members or neighbors who had driven them over, or followed the ambulance. Lots of people took the ambulance even if they weren't hurt very much. They didn't have taxi money, and anybody knew that the doctors saw you faster if you came by ambulance.

Although tonight that did not seem to be the case.

Half the patients waiting had come by ambulance and nobody was calling them back for treatment.

"Hey! Nurse!" yelled a man on Anna Maria's left. "How long I gotta wait here? I been waiting here an hour." His voice lurched a little. He was drunk. Anna Maria managed to scope him out without actually looking in his direction. Unshaven, clothes needing a wash, he had the look of street drunks — angry, confused, potentially dangerous.

"It's busy," the nurse told him. "There are no beds back there."

"I don't care about beds!" The man did not swear, but only because the security guard had straightened up and was staring at him. "They can see me in the hall. Get me in there! Stop screwing around!"

The security guard wandered over.

Anna Maria looked hard at her little sister, and Yasmin obediently changed sides of the table, farther away from the drunk.

The nurse was bored. She had to say this a dozen times a night. "I'm sorry, sir, this is an Emergency Room. We don't see patients in the order they arrive. We see them according to how dangerous their situation is."

"My ankle hurts!' the man bellowed. "You been lettin' people in there all night but you ain't lettin' me in. I gotta die before you look at me?"

The security guard leaned against the wall, right where Yasmin had been sitting. Anna Maria rolled José's stroller closer to the table.

"Since when is a twisted ankle life threatening?" said the nurse. "We've got a motorcycle accident coming in. They will be seen first."

"So how long you tellin' me I gotta wait?" The man left his seat and staggered toward the nurse. He bumped hard against Anna Maria's seat. "Huh? How long? Don't tell me no lies. How long?"

The security guard walked next to the guy.

The two fat gossiping women one row away said to Anna Maria, "Little girl, where's yo' mama at? Who you here with?"

Anna Maria smiled widely and pretended not to speak English.

She knew the fat women were worried about her, but this was not the time for somebody to get involved. This was the time to be invisible.

A burst of laughter rattled out of the television on the wall, and the fat women were distracted.

Anna Maria sneaked a look around to make sure nobody else was wondering where her mama was at.

Nobody was.

ROUTES 14-A AND I-95
6:50 P.M.

With difficulty, the ambulance crew hauled the bike off the teenage boy and exchanged glances. Nothing would be said in front of the patient, but this was a "lock and load." No fancy stuff. They had to get this kid in the ambulance and reach the hospital fast.

They turned the boy over, slid him onto a backboard, and then set the backboard on the narrow stretcher. Heavy cervical collars were put around the boy's neck, to prevent movement. Lifting the stretcher up into the ambulance, the men grunted at the weight, but braced themselves and held steady, trying not to tilt the boy, which would just scare him more. His heart was already racing like a house afire.

The stretcher slid into place and the floor locks automatically snapped onto the stretcher wheels, so it wouldn't roll during the drive — which was not going to be leisurely.

Police waited for the EMTs to signal; they would block traffic so the ambulance could make a U-turn, take the other turnpike entrance, and begin the nine-mile trek to the hospital.

The boy had to be flat on his back, neck unmoving, in case he had injured his spinal cord, but there was also danger of compromising his airway now that he was no longer facedown. The instant that the stretcher was in the ambulance, one EMT sat in the CPR seat and began suction. "It's okay, son," he said soothingly, although it was not.

"What's in his mouth?' asked the second EMT.

"Gravel. Teeth. Blood."

A clear plastic tube, exactly like the suction tube the dentist uses for saliva, but much larger, sucked up the debris that filled Alec's mouth and deposited it in a container that looked exactly like a Mr. Coffee pot.

Alec could feel the suction. It not only took the junk out of his mouth, it took the air. His lungs were being deflated.

The ambulance doors slammed.

The siren began.

Alec convulsed at the two sudden huge noises and the EMT said, "Not to worry, kiddo. Everything's going fine."

Alec could not talk with the thing in his mouth. He could see, though. Blurry faces leaned over, while huge hands crossed his vision like expanded sign language.

He felt movement as the ambulance turned around, and it was not like a car's turn at all, but like an amusement park ride. A whipping dizziness.

They were cutting off his clothes.

Scissors cut through his jeans and underpants.

He was going to be naked in front of these strangers. One of whom was a woman.

He wanted to tell them to stop, that his legs were fine, that he didn't want them to take his jeans off, please, no!

There seemed to be nothing left of the T-shirt. Road burn had reduced his shirt, his chest, and right arm to one big scrape.

"Jeans held up pretty well," said the EMT. "What brand are these?"

"Sneakers didn't make it," said the other one, cutting off what was left of Alec's high tops.

A cold slimy slab covered the agonizing burn where the exhaust pipe had cooked off his skin. Alec moaned slightly and the EMT said, "It's Jell-pac, son. It'll cool off the burn and keep it nice and clean for the doctors to look at."

A tiny clear plastic bag covered his face now, and an explosion of clarity fireworked in his head.

"How much oxygen are you giving him?" said one.

"Fifteen liters. You think that's too high?"

"Nope. That's what I'd do." This EMT said gently, "We're going to pour water over you, son. Get the worst of the junk off your skin. You got sand and pebbles and tar stuck to you. Hang on, this won't feel good."

It didn't.

"You're gonna feel a little stab," said the woman EMT. "I'm starting an IV on your left hand."

He wanted to watch but could see only her moving shoulders and arms. She was braced against the shiny built-in cupboards that lined the interior of the ambulance. He felt nothing when she claimed to be putting in the needle. That scared him more than if he had felt everything.

"He's got a wallet," said the man who had cut off his jeans. "Driver's license says this is Alexander Whitman. Age seventeen."

Distinctly, over everything else, Alec heard a pencil scrawling on paper. They are filling in forms for me, he thought.

He wondered if there were carbons to give to the morgue.

"Taking a corner!" yelled a voice from the front.

He had forgotten about the driver, forgotten how fast they were going.

He felt the engine back off, saw the woman grab a ceiling rod like a subway bar for balance. He felt every degree of the turn the ambulance took. The vehicle whirled. He felt like a vegetable in a blender.

Vegetable.

A picture of himself — unspeaking, unmoving, naked and helpless — appeared in Alec's mind.

Vegetable.

Please, no. Please don't let me be a vegetable.

Emergency Room
6:55 P.M.

Seth was coming back from the Blood Lab, two buildings away. Newly built hospitals would have delivery systems with pneumatic tubes, like drive-up windows of banks, but this hospital was too old and had too many buildings for a straight shoot. Seth loved going to the Blood Lab, not because he got to do anything or talk to anybody, but because the route involved an underground tunnel not accessible to the public.

It was one of the few things he would do tonight where he felt part of the system. Somebody who knew what was going on; a grown-up. He loved that tunnel.

Fat yellow tiles covered the walls and floor of this sub-basement tunnel, but the ceiling, which contained everything that let the hospital exist, was not enclosed. Spookily low over Seth's head stretched armloads of exposed wiring, huge square air-conditioning ducts, and black plastic water mains. This allowed the maintenance crew to reach everything easily, but if you really wanted to disable the hospital, it wouldn't take long from here.

Seth dodged several large carts of dirty laundry being hauled behind a small electric truck. He found the right stairs (elevators were too slow) and walked swiftly back to the ER. (Real doctors did not take their time; they rushed; Seth loved rushing.)

The doors to the Trauma Room were closed and the halls were mobbed by police and ambulance personnel. Something big went down, thought Seth, and I missed it!

Perhaps there had been a drug war or a race riot or a multiple car crash! Seth wedged between the phalanx of cops and reached out for the silvery handle of the Trauma Room door. A cop blocked his way. "Run along, kid."

Run along, kid? The cop was dull looking. Beefy, beer-bellied, in need of a shave. How could this person push Seth around? Seth glared at him, ready to argue, but the cop never even glanced at Seth, never had looked at him to start with; Seth was nothing but a pink jacket taking up valuable space.

The cops passed him like a plate in a restaurant down the hall and out of the way. Oh, well, he thought, diverting himself by looking for the really pretty medical student. He searched the main halls and then poked around through the minor halls that led to X-ray and storage and conference rooms. On his second pass Meggie said, "They're in the Family Room."

"Who?" said Seth.

"The medical students. You think I didn't see you pretending to be one? You want to catch up, they're in the Family Room."

There was a glint in Meggie's eye that Seth could not decipher. He debated his strategy. Should he acknowledge that he had his eye on the pretty doctor? Or did this have nothing to do with flirting? And was there something terrific going on in the Family Room that he should get in on? What was Meggie's motive here? Was she making a gift to him or setting him up?

"You're gonna make a good doctor," Meggie said. "I can see the calculating going on behind your eyes."

I hate women, thought Seth. They spend all their time trying to look inside men. Analyzing us. Trespassing on our thoughts.

Meggie laughed. "Not a bad night for a future doctor. You got three women making eyes at you."

Three? That would have to include Diana. Seth, although busy hating women, found that he was still very interested in them. Playing for time and hoping for clues, he said, "So what's happening in the Family Room?"

"Patient is brain-dead but not body dead. Doctors are telling the family. They got to decide whether to donate the organs and pull the plug or what. Medical students are down there listening to see what kinds of things you say and what kinds of reactions you get."

Seth almost gagged. The family of some half-dead person had to have this terrible announcement made in the company of medical students taking notes on their clipboards?

"This is a teaching hospital," said Meggie. She sounded as if she were quoting a news release. "So anything that happens, you have to expect it to be a teaching event." Meggie adjusted everything on her person. She adjusted her hair, her eyeglasses, her bra straps and the contents of her bra. If Seth did that much adjusting to *his* person, somebody would arrest him. "Go on down there," Meggie added. "You might learn the really good stuff if you go down there." There was such a taunt in her voice that Seth knew it was some kind of test.

I learned something from Diana, he thought. I think I know the passing grade here. He sat down next to Meggie. The inner side of the desk was usually littered with doctors using telephones or computers, scribbling on charts, or looking something up in the pharmacology references. It was rare to find an empty seat. What great stuff had he missed? Seth looked longingly at the press of cops blocking the

Trauma Room and forced himself to pay attention to Meggie. "I guess I don't want to interrupt the family, Meggie," he said, although in a sick and twisted way he wanted very much to do that. "I guess that's pretty hard on the family."

Meggie relaxed. She smiled at him. He had passed her test, and Meggie thought better of him.

Diana was walking in their direction, very slowly for Diana, a sheet of paper in her hand. She was about the same color as the sheet of paper. Seth frowned.

Meggie said to Seth, so casually that he knew it was not casual at all, "What're you doing tonight after work?"

A hundred thoughts rocketed through Seth's mind. None were complimentary to Meggie. Was she asking him out? What if somebody saw him with her? How could she possibly think — but when he looked her way, he knew she had thought he would be interested, and he could not imagine how to be polite about his refusal. He could hardly answer, "Ugh! Yuck! Never!"

After all, no matter what night of the week he volunteered here, Meggie would still control the desk; he had to stay friends with her. Now how was he supposed to accomplish that without notice or time to prepare an intelligent answer?

Since Meggie worked the four-to-midnight

shift, he said, "Diana and I are probably quitting around nine and we have to share a taxi back to the dorm. I haven't even started studying yet, so I'll probably be up until one or two hitting the books. My roommates will throw old sandwich crusts at me to make me turn out the lights." He laughed lightly, pretending he and Meggie shared the trials of being a college kid.

Meggie of course saw right through him, going back to her original assessment of Seth as calculating.

Women stuck together. They never considered them*selves* calculating. Oh, no. Only men. We just calculate differently, he thought.

He tried to saunter off, but under Meggie's stare, every move was awkward. Diana was almost upon them, walking with a queer lurch, as if the paper she held in her hand weighed a great deal.

What if Meggie told Diana about the supposed taxi sharing? Diana didn't want to share Seth's oxygen, never mind a backseat. Well, the thing was to distract everybody. "Hey, Diana," he teased, "you look as if you've been asked to escort a body to the morgue."

Diana's black hair looked even blacker, and her skin even whiter, as if she were human no longer, but had been cut out of paper. "Seth." Diana said his name as if it were a key. A door. "Seth, I have to show you something."

He could not help himself. "Gee, Diana, thing is, I'm in a hurry. Stuff I do is important, you know."

"Okay," she said, "I know I've been kind of — well — "

"A bitch," said Meggie.

Both Seth and Diana blinked. "Well . . ." said Diana, flushing, but not using the word herself. She took Seth by the sleeve, and he wanted her to hold his arm, not the cloth; he wanted her to put her hand on his waist or his cheek, not his elbow. She pulled him into an ell where ceiling-height open-wire carts stored IV bottles, disposable thermometers, sheets, blankets, urinals, Kleenex, and gloves.

Seth made a mental note of the spot, in case any pretty medical students or Diana wanted to do something other than air kiss.

"*Seth.*"

She was actually trembling. He could not believe this. The Dianas of the world did not quiver. "What's wrong?" he felt himself changing from future doctor to Diana's brother. I don't want to be her brother, he thought.

"Volunteer!" yelled Meggie from around the corner.

Not now, Meggie, he thought. But, of course, now was when Meggie would yell for them.

"Seth," said Diana again, heavily, as if she needed the name. "The man in Bed Eight."

Seth waited for her to go on but she didn't. She looked glazed. "Yeah?" he said. "The white guy? About fifty? Shortness of breath?"

She nodded.

"What did he do to you?" asked Seth, suddenly angry, suddenly ready to go in there and slam the guy against the wall.

She held out the paper, presumably the guy's insurance stuff. But she didn't look at it. Her face trembled, and the smile she put on was unconnected to her thoughts. It came to Seth that if he had ever needed a bedside manner, he needed it now. Hesitantly, Seth put an arm around her shoulders. Diana did not appear to notice it there, which made him feel supremely awkward. He did not know how to touch in a comforting fashion. Perhaps he should practice. "Tell me what's wrong," he said. Now he didn't even like the sound of his voice. Not soothing at all, but kind of rough. He should practice that, too. Make his voice kind. How did you do that, if you weren't basically a kind person?

What if I'm not kind enough? thought Seth. What if Diana's right? What if I really am in this for power and prestige and money and pushing people around? What if Meggie and Knika are right, and I'm just another despicable would-be doctor?

"What did Bed Eight do?" repeated Seth.

"I think," said Diana Dervane, "that he's my father."

THE SECOND HOUR

THE CITY
7:00 P.M.

"Mother?" said Roo nervously. She tugged on her own long hair, as if this would give her courage. "Do you think you could help me with the twins tonight?"

"No."

The syllable hit Roo like a slap on the face. It was intended that way. Roo trembled. She needed an ally so badly she could not think. "Mother, I'm really coming apart. Please help me."

"We've been through this, Ruth. You had choices. You made them. You have to live with it."

"It's too hard!" she cried. "Mother, it's too hard!"

"You should have thought of that."

She was five miles from her mother. Not in the pretty suburb but the terrifying welfare housing of the City. Not in the comfortable ranch house with its two bathrooms and easy-to-clean linoleum kitchen, but in an ugly dark apartment with roaches. It might as well have been five hundred miles. She had no car. Thursdays, her mother grimly did her good deed, and took Roo and the twins grocery shopping and then to canvas every thrift shop they could find for clothing for the babies. The City had a good bus system, but managing the double stroller by herself was impossible.

On nice days she stuck the twins in the stroller and walked. At first the street terrified her. After all these months, she was far more terrified, having seen what the City could be, but if she stayed home she became angry.

The anger was different from anything Roo had ever felt. It was creeping violence. It would begin in her fingertips and crawl back upward into her hands. Then her hands would knot into fists and she would have to wrap her arms around herself to keep from hitting the twins. The desire to hit the twins lived in her own hands, like evil muscles that belonged to some other body; some wrestler's or boxer's body.

But it was Roo's.

Cal and Val cried all the time. They had diarrhea. Their noses ran. If one slept, the other was awake. They messed up everything. The floor of the little apartment was never free of stuffed toys or tipped-over plastic juice glasses.

She had thought their names were so cute when she picked them out: Callum and Valerie. Now they were nonsense syllables. Cal and Val. Like her life. She could not make sense of her life.

The babies were impossible to escape.

Roo kept the television on twenty-four hours a day. It was her only friend.

Today had been unbearably hot and the arrival of evening had not cooled the apartment one degree. The apartment baked. The babies screamed. Their diaper rashes got worse and their eyes watered and —

Maybe they have fevers! thought Roo eagerly.

She could go to the Emergency Room. It would be air-conditioned. The nurses would take the babies. Roo would duck out and go to the cafeteria. She had a couple of dollars. She could get a Pepsi. Sit in that cool clean dining hall and listen to people talk about their work.

She thought of her old friends. Amy would be playing a softball game against JFK High. Lucy would be at the pool wearing her newest bikini for her newest boyfriend. Megan would be at the mall with her allowance. Doing what seventeen-year-old girls did.

Roo forced herself to change diapers yet again. Then she filled two bottles with milk from the refrigerator, stuffing them into the carry bag latched to the back of the stroller, and strapped the twins in, thinking, What lie will I tell the nurse? I'll say their fevers were a hundred and one.

It's the City Hospital. They can't say no.

EMERGENCY ROOM
7:01 P.M.

Seth knew his father pretty well. They'd tossed baseballs back and forth since Seth was a tot. Shared many a pizza and math assignment. Had had fierce arguments and gone to a million movies together. Keeping the house alive had been their mutual assignment: They were evermore patching the roof, changing the lightbulbs, mowing the lawn, arguing over how the plastic Christmas tree came apart.

When his parents divorced, Seth had thought it would kill him; but his parents had been good — if anybody is ever good during a divorce — and he saw both his mother and father whenever he wanted. More than anything else, Seth had hated the new purchases that went with any divorce. Getting another fake Christmas tree for the parent who didn't inherit the original one. Replacing the CD player the other parent kept. Buying another big casserole to cook the lasagne in at the new place.

But that, thankfully, had been two years before college. He felt safe about the two houses he had now, the two separated parents, the new sets of china, and the new lawnmower. He knew exactly where his father and mother were because they were involved in a post-divorce game of seeing who could keep in touch with Seth the most.

So Seth did not know what to make of Diana's shaky sentence. How could you just "think" somebody was your father? Wasn't that the kind of thing you knew for sure? Didn't you know this over the course of your eighteen years, six million arguments, twenty thousand photographs, and six thousand good night hugs?

"Volunteer!" came Meggie's outraged screech.

"My father's name was Rob Searle," said Diana. "He left when I was four to marry somebody else. My mother took back her maiden name for both of us. We never heard from my father again. He never paid child support. He never wrote, never sent a Christmas card, never sent a birthday present."

Seth felt as if his mind were too full; it was actually overflowing. This was not a good sign. How was he going to learn all the facts required of him in medical school if he ran out of brain space in one conversation with Diana Dervane? "You think that's him? In Bed Eight?"

She nodded.

"Let's kill him," said Seth.

Diana actually laughed. "When your first thought is homicide, you've been in the ER too long."

"A guy that doesn't send his baby girl birthday presents? A guy that lets her grow up without even being able to recognize him in the street? Or the hospital bed?" Seth shook his head. "Kill him, I say."

"I think there are a couple people in the Waiting Room who have weapons to lend us."

"Heck, let's just hire them. They probably need the money. What's he worth to you, this father? I have enough cash to buy a candy bar. Or off the guy in Bed Eight."

"This is the sickest conversation I have ever had in my life," said Diana. But she was giggling.

"He's sicker," pointed out Seth.

"You mean mentally," said Diana, "but he's also sick physically. That's why he's here."

"Let's check out his next of kin," said Seth. "This wife might be in the Waiting Room. What was her name, do you remember?"

"Bunny."

"No way," said Seth. "Nobody is named Bunny."

"It probably wasn't her real name. It was probably a nickname. Her real name was probably Gertrude or something. But I don't necessarily want to do anything, Seth."

"You think this patient could be your biological father and you're not sure whether you're going to talk to the guy or introduce yourself or anything?" Seth was dying to know, and it wasn't his father!

"What would I say?" Diana asked him.

"How about, 'Hi, I'm your daughter Diana, who you haven't seen in fifteen years, and I have a lethal dose of poison for you.'?"

"Stop that! You pervert! I don't want him to die. I want . . ."

Her voice drifted off. She didn't know what she wanted.

Seth knew what he wanted. Diana. She might just be the prettiest girl at the entire college. Although that medical student was in the running for prettiest girl at the hospital.

He knew he shouldn't say girl. He should say woman. But he didn't like saying woman because it sounded too competitive. Girl sounded more controllable. Then he hated himself for wanting to control Diana. *She* would certainly hate him for it.

"How can I help?" said Seth. There. Success. Just the voice he wanted. Sexy, but comforting. He tightened the arm that was lying on her shoulder, in what he hoped would be a friendly fashion.

She took the hand off, as if it were a scarf, and like a scarf twisted his fingers around hers. He liked it. Her hands were cool and smooth and her fingernails felt neat, glossy clear polish sliding against his skin.

"Oh, Volunteer?" said Meggie, having actually left her desk and walked around to find them. Meggie was not fond of exercise, and leaving her swivel chair was an awesome amount of activity for her.

Seth opened his mouth to tell Meggie he was busy, but she saw the words coming. "Busy, huh? Typical. You college kids come down here, show off a little, try to rack up points with your professors, do good, that kind of crap. And then you — "

"What do you need?" interrupted Seth. "Name it, we do it. Seth — and/or Diana — at your service!" He gave her his biggest, finest grin but Meggie simply looked at Diana.

Meggie hated Diana, it was in her eyes. Seth all but shivered. What's that about? he thought.

It never crossed his mind that it was about him.

"They need that guy's paperwork," Meggie said to Diana.

Seth whipped the insurance sheet out of

Diana's hand and bowed to her. "I shall accomplish this task," he said in his knight-in-shining-armor voice. He could hardly wait to stare down Bed Eight. Check out what kind of guy —

"What do you think you're doing!" hissed Diana, ripping the sheet right back out of his hand. "I'll thank you not to interfere in my life. Or his either! Who do you think you are, you arrogant future doctor, you?"

Seth stared at her. "I was just helping," he protested.

"It's my own fault for saying a single thing to you," said Diana, furiously, and he thought how grand she looked — really regal — in her rage. Not whiny, not minor, but immense, as if Diana's fury could blow the walls down.

"Stop smiling!" shouted Diana. "It is so sick the way you take such pleasure in other people's troubles."

She stomped away, and now his attention was taken by the wonderful switch of her walk.

Meggie said, "Guess you're not sharing a taxi after all, huh, Seth?"

Oh, no! She was going to invite him out again. Seth said hastily, "I think they need me in Trauma, Meggie."

EMERGENCY ROOM
7:10 P.M.

The hallways were so crowded that neither Seth nor Diana could pass. Stretchers bumped into stretchers and portable X-ray units and treatment trays and wheelchairs snagged on people's legs.

They were rolling one of the GSWs out of the Trauma Room.

The girl from college. I forgot her! thought Diana. She might be dying and instead of thinking about her, and worrying about her, or praying for her, I'm all worked up about some man who — if he's my father — never got worked up enough about me to send a birthday card.

The girl was just paler than she had been, and becoming fidgety, her finger knotting and searching the bed. Jersey. That was her name. She roomed with Susan and Mai.

"Systolic blood pressure is dropping," said one nurse impassively to another. Jersey was going into shock; blood loss was causing her body to shut down whatever it could in an attempt to save whatever it could.

Rolled blankets had been packed along Jersey's body to keep her on her side. While a medical student held her IVs aloft so gravity would keep them running, and the tech rolled the portable heart monitor alongside, a doctor and two nurses wheeled the stretcher toward the patient elevators. They must be taking her to the operating room.

Briefly, the doors to the Trauma Room remained open.

Where Jersey's stretcher had been, and where her blood had spilled, the floor was not red, but yellow. Footprints of Jersey's blood tracked out of the room and down the hall. The housekeeping staff mopped up.

"Everything's fine, sweetie," said the nurse to Jersey, patting her hair. "Everything's going to be all right. You've got excellent surgeons waiting for you. Wang and Seredy, they're the best."

Let it be, thought Diana. Let Wang and Seredy be the best and let it all be all right for Jersey.

She slid a little on the yellow slick of Jersey's blood, and swallowed hard before she went back to Insurance.

Mary didn't even ask why Diana didn't want

to do Bed 8, but just nodded, took the paperwork, and set off to interview Mr. Searle.

Diana tried asking herself why she didn't
want to do Bed 8, but it was too much. She
literally could not think about it.

She could not think about Seth, either. Why
must she always lash out at him? How did other
girls just enjoy boys? How did they relax and
flirt? Why was she either at war or at a loss?

EMERGENCY ROOM
7:16 P.M.

The mob of police had thinned out. The ER was rather like the ocean, with schools of fish coming and going. Groups of cops or doctors or student nurses or sobbing families were swept in and out, as if by tides, and where they went or where they came from was often hard to tell.

Seth stationed himself at the ambulance bay to see the motorcycle accident come in. Trauma would want him around in case they needed an errand done, but if they didn't, he'd get to watch.

The victim was almost completely covered with sheets, and there were four EMTs, one at each side of the stretcher, rushing him straight into the Trauma Room, so basically he saw nothing.

Seth was irked. No fair covering up. He tried to remember that somebody was in agony under that sheet. Who was Seth to want to gape and stare and calculate the man's chances?

I'm a future doctor, that's who I am, thought Seth. Calculating as they come, or so I'm told.

He followed the stretcher into Trauma.

The Trauma team was ready, having had perhaps five minutes between the GSWs and this MVA. When the sheet was lifted, there was much less blood than Seth expected. Basically the body was shredded from the waist up, looked fairly okay from the waist down, and the face was no longer very facial.

Ambulance attendants hovered around, frowning over clipboards, trying to fill in their various forms. There was more form-filling at City Hospital than body-healing. Seth looked over the EMT's shoulder to see what was being checked off.

If vehicular, was victim — driver? passenger? pedestrian?

Trauma source — sharp object? blunt object? firearm? toxin/drug?

Source — contact sport? fight/violence? machinery? self-inflicted?

Seth hoped shortly to witness some machinery, sharp object, and fight/violence stuff. Then he glanced at the man's date of birth.

The man was one year younger than Seth. He was a kid. He'd be in high school!

Seth looked away from the pieces of paper and back at the real patient. The boy was naked, although somebody had ineffectively flung a sheet over his lower body. He was now hooked up to two portable monitors and had two IVs running.

The nurses were scrubbing the boy's torn flesh with an actual brush, getting the tar and pebbles and sand out. The way you would scrub a broiler pan with baked-on drippings. Hard.

The doctor was a thin, gray-haired woman. "What shall I call you, son?" said the doctor. "Alex?"

"Alec," said the boy, mumbling through his terribly damaged mouth. "Am I dying?"

"I hope not, Alec," she said. "But flesh and bone don't do well when it hits pavement at that speed. We'll do what we can."

Seth was shocked. Why hadn't the doctor reassured this kid? What was with that little lecture? It was late in the day to bother warning him about the effects of pavement on skin. She looked kind and grandmotherly, and here she was letting this kid lie there all bare and exposed to wonder if he was dying!

"Blood gas," called somebody.

Blood gas was an analysis to gauge the levels

of things like oxygen, nitrogen, and carbon monoxide in the patient's blood, but Seth did not know how it was done nor why a special technician was called. He watched closely.

The tech took the patient's wrist firmly and bent it backward, until the tendons and small bones were visible. A two-inch needle was stuck between the bones deep down into the wrist. The tech wasn't getting blood from a vein — one of the blue lines along the surface — but from an artery, safely hidden deep within the body. Getting arterial blood was no picnic for the patient.

It took the tech three tries, during which Seth winced more than the boy on the bed.

Blood began to fill the large tube attached to the needle. To Seth's horror and shame, his stomach began to roil. He swallowed hard, trying to control his gut.

"Get out," said a nurse, moving him swiftly to the door. "Don't even think about throwing up in here." She went out with him and shut the door behind them both, firmly. In the relatively dull hall, away from the sight and smell of Trauma, his stomach calmed and he could pretend he hadn't been about to vomit over the doctors' feet. The nurse washed her hands at the wall sink. Handwashing was so continual that lots of people carried their own hand lotion around with them.

"Why did the doctor talk to the motorcycle accident so roughly?" Seth asked her.

"Roughly? Dr. Gold?" The nurse was startled. "She's wonderful."

"She didn't reassure him that he wouldn't die."

"We don't lie anymore," said the nurse. "We used to, twenty years ago. But it's his life and if he just ended it, he has a right to know."

THE WAITING ROOM
7:30 P.M.

The Admitting Nurse looked at Roo without any expression whatsoever. "Possible fever?" Barbie repeated. She was not sarcastic. She was not anything. She was just a nurse who then took the twins' temperatures. They had no temperatures. "It'll be a long wait tonight," she said to the mother. "Do you have a private doctor you can call?"

Roo shook her head.

Barbie shrugged. She filled out separate sheets for Cal and for Val. The top sheet would go to the Pediatric ER so the doctors there could decide when to see the babies. The bottom sheet would go to Insurance. Barbie had made her own decision about the importance of these illnesses: Of the three boxes (Immediate, Urgent, Nonurgent), both Cal and Val were checked Nonurgent.

Roo read the handwriting upside down. "Mother claims fever."

So the nurse knew perfectly well that there was no fever. Roo turned quickly away, unable to meet the nurse's eyes. Luckily a pale and sweating woman with a sliced-open palm was right there, dropping into the patient's chair with a thud of need. The nurse now had better things to do than consider Roo.

Nonurgent patients, Roo knew from experience, might truly wait hours. Your runny nose did not ever come ahead of your gunshot wound. Since she hadn't come in order to be seen anyhow, Roo was willing to wait hours. Strangers found the twins adorable and the Waiting Room held at least four middle-aged women who could be coaxed to hold a twin.

Just to be out of that terrible apartment gave Roo hope that she could endure. That somehow she would get through the summer and the twins would get easier and life would not be so very terrible.

Of course it was only May. Summer had yet to begin.

When Roo was pregnant and refused to say who the father was, her own parents had said, "Do you understand that if you have this baby, it will be *for eighteen years*? Do you understand that? You aren't even eighteen yet yourself!"

Well, she had had two of them, and no, she

had not dreamed how hard it would be for eighteen *days*, never mind eighteen years.

Well, forget that.

Roo set to work on two black women whose mama had had a heart attack and who were waiting to talk to the doctor. They were happy to chat. They watched as much TV as Roo did and the three women traded opinions of talk-show hosts.

Val got whiny. She was always the first to get whiny. Roo said to her new friends, "I'm so tired of holding her. I mean, there are two of them. I just get so tired."

"Would you let me hold her?" asked one, right on cue. "I love babies."

Yes! thought Roo, handing Val over.

Immediately Cal began screaming. Jealousy definitely began with birth.

The second woman looked knowingly at Roo, and Roo knew that they knew what was going on. Perhaps they had been there themselves, or seen it before. But they knew, and willingly they bailed her out for a while, cuddling the twins. She wanted to fling herself upon their soft breasts and be comforted, too.

Of all the things Roo had not understood when she was pregnant, most of all she had not understood that she would never be first again. The babies would always come first. She had not known what discipline it would take — dis-

cipline she lacked — to put her children first
and set herself aside time and again.

But for a few minutes, Roo didn't have to
think heavy thoughts.

She was light and young and airy again. Bur-
dens lifted

At a low table sat two small Puerto Rican
girls, coloring. Their little brother was in a
stroller, the cheap sack-type, in which his little
body was folded up like a loaf of soft bread.
Roo was amazed to find herself actually worrying about somebody else's baby, about his
spine, whether it was good for him to sit like
that.

The little girls colored furiously.

Roo had been so good in art. Mr. Hanrahan
had always wanted her to go to college for art.
Why, sophomore year Roo had designed post-
ers for every event in school. The musical, the
dance club's performance, model UN, Ecology
Day . . .

Junior year, of course, she spent giving
birth.

Roo looked longingly at the crayon table. An
old paper cup held maybe a dozen crayons. All
the good colors were gone. But there was a
stack of white paper, waiting.

She didn't ask permission. The ladies might
say no. She just left Cal and Val with them,
slid over four or five seats and took one of the

tiny oak chairs around the table. "Hi," she said to the little girls.

They said nothing back but smiled sweetly.

"What are you making?" she said. "Castles? Oooh, that one's pretty. I'll make a castle, too." She took the navy crayon and in moments her castle covered three overlapping sheets, full of courtyards, knights, moats, flags, towers, and crenellated bastions. The little girls were awestruck.

The smaller one spread her finger wide on a sheet of fresh paper and slid the paper and her hand toward Roo.

Roo traced the tiny hand and then drew wonderful rings and bracelets and a beautiful watch. She made long terrifying fingernails and they colored the fingernails green because they had no pink or red.

The Waiting Room surged and changed.

People tired of wondering when their turn would come and just went home without ever being seen by a doctor.

Families got hungry and went to the cafeteria.

Taxis arrived to take discharged patients home.

Friends wandered in, found the place was closed to visitors, and wandered away.

Security guards came and went. All they

ever did was make sure nobody smoked inside, or showed drivers where short-term parking was, or coaxed staggering drunks to leave. Nobody felt threatened by them, or even interested.

The big outer doors, opened by an electronic eye, admitted two very gaudily dressed young men.

Trouble.

The electronic eye saw only height, and opened its doors for anything above three feet. Human eyes, turning toward the motion, saw much more than height.

Anna Maria looked down at her paper and colored hard. The atmosphere of the room changed. People were stilled. Their eyes ceased to roam and their pages ceased to turn. Nobody was sure anymore what they were waiting for. Several decided they weren't so sick after all, and when Trouble moved toward the turquoise chairs behind the coloring table, those patients drifted casually toward the exit.

Members of KSI. About half the room knew what kind of money they made, and how they made it, and what cars they drove, and what weapons they used. The other half of the room could make a good guess.

José was too little to draw any conclusions. He dropped his bottle and the loss of it started him screaming. Grown-ups hated screaming babies. Drug dealers were especially irritable grown-ups. They would really hate screaming babies. Anna Maria bent down quickly, retrieved the bottle, and popped it into José's mouth. She prayed to the Lord Jesus that that would shut José up.

She knew one of them. Dunk. She did not know if he liked the nickname or hated it, so she would never have taken the risk of using it.

Dunk was her mother's age. Maybe twenty-three or four. He had the kind of white complexion that does not look finished: too white. Bread that needed more time in the toaster. He was thin — rail thin, sick thin — but at the same time, he was puffy from his own drug use. His face and throat were bloated like a rotting fish. He was immaculately groomed. Jewelry gathered at the open collar of his beautiful shirt. His tight-fitting pants, shiny with gold-and-black threads on a white background, fit him so closely that what he carried in his pockets was outlined as if Anna Maria had crayoned it on the cloth.

A bulge as round as a hamburger roll filled his left pocket. Anna Maria knew it was a roll of dollars. Sometimes he added her mother's money to that roll.

In the other pocket, sagging heavily, was a handgun.

Anna Maria kept her head down and continued filling in the green grass on her farm picture. Next to her, the pretty young mother was oblivious — had seen nothing, had understood nothing. Anna Maria often felt older than older people, and she did now — worrying that the young mother would do something stupid.

There was a reason why they didn't allow visitors in the treatment area when there had been a gunshot wound. Drug dealers never shot in order to wound somebody; they shot to kill. A wound was a mistake. Mistakes could be corrected.

Anna Maria did not mind at all if drug dealers killed each other.

But she minded a lot if she and Yasmin and José got in the middle.

Every security guard had headed for the ambulance bay. The nurse was examining an incoming patient (a young black boy who had broken his leg playing baseball, eager to have a really good heavy cast to show off in school); on the phone with a patch; and holding a second phone with a doctor wanting to question her.

The Waiting Room was jammed with people. But for a few minutes it was oddly unprotected. Unsupervised.

Anna Maria added a row of tulips to the bottom of her drawing. The young mother added a princess in a beautiful flowing gown.

Two feet away, Dunk and his partner took their time. Doctors rushed, nurses rushed, ambulances rushed, but drug dealers took their time. Nobody pushed them. They had time to swagger and show off. Nobody got in their way. And people that did ended up on the pavement, while their blood spurted out of them.

"Let's draw wedding gowns," said the pretty young mother to Anna Maria. Anna Maria continued to pretend she spoke no English, but she watched as the wedding gown materialized from the stubby green crayon. She knows nothing, thought Anna Maria. She's stupid. I'm stupid, too, for coming here.

We have to get out of here.

EMERGENCY ROOM
7:37 P.M.

I might be paralyzed, thought Alec, but I'm no vegetable. That is a really cute girl.

He looked up at her, genuinely distracted from his pain and fear. She was so pretty. Short crisp black hair was like artwork. Large hazel eyes, wide with worry for Alec. Ruddy cheeks, hot pink. She loomed over him, even though she was small. Lying down gave Alec such different perspectives. Faces were huge. Bodies were mainly shoulders and breasts.

"Mr. Whitman?" she said. She flinched a little, looking at him.

How bad is it, he thought, that she can't look at me?

"He can't talk with the airway," said somebody. "Here's his wallet. Go through it and get what you can."

He could see how reluctant she was to go through his wallet.

There was nothing in there but his driver's license and a few dollars. He had no credit cards. He wasn't old enough. Alec could not see what they were doing. The collar that kept him from moving his neck also kept him from seeing anything that wasn't directly above him. He felt like a horse wearing blinders. Many people moved around him, but he could see only their heads, not what their hands were doing.

The room spun a little and he wondered if he would get old enough for credit cards. Was this dying — this spinning around? Or just plain old dizziness, nothing to sweat?

THE WAITING ROOM
7:40 P.M.

Trouble stood up and swaggered toward the Admitting Nurse. He shot his cuffs and thrust his skinny ankles out to show off his beautiful boots. His watch glittered on his wrist.

Anna Maria watched from behind her long dark eyelashes.

"I wanna see Tillotson," said Dunk.

"Tillotson?" repeated the nurse, not looking up from her paperwork. She cradled a phone against her cheek but did not talk into it.

"He got shot. I gotta be with him."

"No visitors right now," said the nurse, looking up. She had no more expression on her face than when Roo claimed the twins had had fevers.

"Tillotson's my brother," said Dunk.

The nurse surveyed Dunk's pasty white skin. "He's black," she said.

Dunk grinned. A gold-and-scarlet emblem

had been glued to one of his front teeth. "You got a problem with that?" said Dunk.

The Waiting Room listened, both entertained and afraid.

"No visitors right now," repeated the nurse, shifting her gum to the other side of her mouth. "Hospital rule. No visitors when there's a gunshot wound."

Dunk stabbed his long fingers at the nurse. "I gotta be with him."

"No. No visitors." The nurse began speaking into her phone. She was describing a festering wound that should have come for treatment days ago but had waited and now would need a plastic surgeon.

Dealers walked and waited with a special sway. They owned the street and they owned their customers and it was in their feet and their stride. Dunk stood as if he owned the linoleum and the hospital.

But he didn't. The nurse did.

Dunk left the admitting desk slowly, controlling his anger and yet letting it roll out over the Waiting Room, so everybody there could see it, and feel it, and panic about it. If he couldn't make the nurse tremble, he could see to it that the rest of them did.

Anna Maria was afraid no security guard would come and afraid that one would. She was afraid to go back to coloring and afraid to get up and move the stroller.

THE WAITING ROOM
7:42 P.M.

After the motorcycle accident, Diana had a homeless woman brought in by the police. Ankles grotesquely swollen, feet half covered by torn moccasins that did not match, thick legs encased in several pairs of stockings rolled up below the knees.

Once she was in school, thought Diana. Once she took spelling tests and went to basketball games and bought new pencils in September.

"Hi, Norma," said the nurse, shaking the woman's arm.

"You know her?" said Diana.

"Sure. She's a regular. Police check out her favorite corners and bring her in when they need to."

"Why would they need to?"

"When she's drunk as this," said the nurse, "she might hurt herself, or hurt somebody else.

She'll step off a curb and break an ankle because she doesn't see the drop, or she'll step in front of a car, and some poor innocent driver will have killed somebody."

The nurse sounded oddly affectionate and, even more oddly, the cop who had brought Norma in came over and gave the unconscious woman a pat. "We don't worry so much in summer," he confided in Diana. "In winter though, then they could freeze to death, we do our rounds pretty carefully. Don't wanna miss somebody in the dark, let 'em die."

"But — don't they go to shelters?" said Diana.

"Nah. Not when they're as low down as Norma. She forgets. Plus shelters have rules, and Norma can't keep 'em."

"They bring Norma in about every week," said the nurse, telling Diana her last name for the computer. "You'll recognize them, too, pretty soon."

Diana felt curiously honored that both a nurse and a policeman were actually conversing with her. She found the nerve to look down the hall at Bed 8.

It was empty.

No patient. No bed. No nothing.

She wet her lips. "Where's the patient in Eight?" she said to the nurse.

The nurse frowned, trying to remember.

"Radiology, I think. Yes, angiogram. Patient's an MI. Won't be back here for a couple of hours. Why? Is the family asking about him?"

Diana's shock was so great she lost her balance. *Is the family asking about him?* Had that scum Seth betrayed her? Gossiped? Told? Started with Meggie and spread it over the entire ER?

Or could the nurse tell by looking? Was there a physical resemblance between Diana and Bed 8 strong enough for a nurse (with nine other patients to look after) to notice?

But the nurse was not even glancing at Diana. She was already in the clutches of a patient who wanted more attention than he was getting, and who had gotten up off his bed in a grim search for a nurse. "Listen," said the guy, ready to explode, "I spent two hours in that Waiting Room and I've been sitting on the edge of that stupid bed for another forty-five minutes and now — "

"It's terrible, isn't it?" agreed the nurse. "If people didn't keep shooting each other or falling off motorcycles, the staff could get to the rest of you sooner." She took his arm to escort him back to his cubicle. "We just don't have enough doctors to go around, sir. The thing is, gunshot wounds consume so many people that there's nobody to see the rest of the patients."

"But I was here first!" said the man. "This place is such a zoo. I hate this hospital."

"I know what you mean," said the nurse, and behind his back she rolled her eyes for Diana's benefit.

Diana steadied herself against the wall. Its dull, flat, pale-green paint seemed like a friend to rely on. Of course the nurse hadn't seen a family resemblance and of course Seth hadn't told. When the no-visitor rule was in effect, the Waiting Room always had griping family members demanding volunteers to get them past the security guards.

An MI. He'd had a heart attack then, and they were going to shoot dye into his heart to see what was going on.

If he's my father, she thought, he doesn't *have* a heart, and *that's* what's going on.

She had a couple of hours before Bed 8 would matter again. Before she had to make the decision of whether to go in there and find out if *that* Rob Searle was *her* Rob Searle.

Nobody's *my* Rob Searle, she thought. Realistically, I haven't had a Rob Searle since I was four. Do I care if this man who didn't care about me is dying? Should I care? I could be dead, and he wouldn't know.

It occurred to her that since no visitors were allowed in back, and since Bed 8 was two floors and a building away now, that Bunny (Bunny who was better than Mommy, Bunny who took Daddy away forever and ever from both of them) might be in the Waiting Room.

The better to stare at everybody, Diana slid onto one of the toddler seats at the crayoning table.

On holidays, Diana would still catch herself, suddenly aware that she was checking the mail and listening for the phone. Thinking — this birthday, surely, he'll call me up. This Christmas, he'll send a present. This Valentine's Day, he'll send a card.

But there had been no mail, and no phone calls, and no presents.

Sometimes Diana had pretended he was dead. Once when they were eleven, she and her best friend Trace walked to the cemetery and pretended their fathers were under the stones there. It felt so good they decided to hold a burial service. "You're dead!" shouted Trace, jumping up and down on a strip of green, green grass next to a stone with somebody else's name.

Diana and Trace had walked back home, slightly ashamed of themselves, as if they had done something twisted and sick.

Whatever happened to Trace? she thought. We moved away, Trace moved away, I haven't heard from her in years. Maybe I'll try to write again, see if they'll forward the letter. Tracy Stratton, where are you? Do you remember the day we tried to bury our daddies?

Diana's fingers tightened on the crayon.

If I look up, and if I look around, she thought

then, will I see this Bunny, who changed our lives? Is she sitting a few feet away from me, worrying about shortness of breath in the man she took from us?

I'm blaming Bunny, thought Diana clearly. I've always blamed Bunny. But Daddy was a grown-up. Bunny didn't take him. He went. After all these years, I have not accepted that.

Diana Dervane stared down at her coloring.

She had drawn a blue house with a slanted roof and a red chimney. She had curled lots of gray smoke into the sky. She had drawn a mommy, a daddy, and a smiling little girl on the lawn.

After all these years! she thought. I'm still pretending that we are a family of three, not two.

THE WAITING ROOM
7:48 P.M.

Dunk was not in control and he hated it. He had been turned down by some overweight, chain-smoking broad and there was no way past her; the sliding doors would no longer open unless she pressed her floor button. He could not get into the treatment area unless she said he could.

He knew the treatment area well, having been there many times in his brief life. He knew that unlike the doors which stopped him now, the doors to the ambulance bay were always open. There was a guard on the outside but there probably was not a guard on the inside. He knew that the chaos was so great that he could slip in and the face-masked staff would be too busy to even glance up. He knew that the boy he had intended to kill was probably still in Trauma and it would be a simple matter to off him and get out.

It would, in fact, be exciting. Something he had not done before. It would be on TV. It would be daring, and the networks would cover it.

One of the problems KSI lamented was lack of TV coverage. You could be the most violent and visible gang in the City, but if you went and got your own face on TV, which Dunk would have loved, then the police had something to work with. Dunk knew the police well and had been arrested several times. He'd been back on the street in a matter of hours and had never done time.

Dunk had half forgotten why he'd been mad enough to kill Tillotson. Now he was less mad than he was challenged. He wanted to pull this off in spite of City Hospital. Show this stupid nurse and these pathetic play-cops dressed up as "security" that *no* — they were not secure. As long as KSI existed, they'd never be secure. And Dunk was KSI.

He would have to leave the Waiting Room. Walk around the parking area, slip past the pitiful excuse of a guard watching over the cars, come up into the ambulance bay, and get into the treatment area from that direction.

He left the nurse to her phone call. He swaggered past the little kids coloring so furiously, pausing for a moment to admire the prettiness of the young mother who was tracing everybody's hands; he thought what he would do with her if he got her alone.

He lowered himself casually next to his partner, after first displaying himself and his jewelry, and the gun bulging in his pocket, for the Waiting Room to admire. "Here's what we'll do," he murmured.

THE WAITING ROOM
7:49 P.M.

Roo was fascinated by Diana Dervane. Nobody deserved to look that good.

She's got my life, thought Roo. I was supposed to be in college, with time to do good deeds, so I could look beautiful even in a revolting pink volunteer jacket. I was supposed to flirt with doctors and live in a dorm and dance with cute boys.

How had she done this to herself?

The babies' father was long gone. How easy it was for a boy to distance himself. In Andy's case, the distance was several hundred miles and an unlisted phone number. She had obeyed his wish not to be officially listed as the father. He had said he would always take care of the baby anyway. He had never done a thing. "Well, if you hadn't had twins," Andy had said irritably, "maybe I could do this child-support stuff. But two of them? Come on, be real."

I'm being real, thought Roo, and I don't think much of it.

She turned around to see how the twins were doing. They were back in their double stroller. Cal was asleep and Val was sucking her thumb, staring up at the ceiling lights. The black women had left.

I want to leave, too! thought Roo.

What would the world do to her if she were just to abandon the children? She could. All the money and identification Roo had in the world was in her purse. She didn't have to go back to that awful apartment. She could take a bus from here to the train station and a train to anywhere. Roo could wait tables, or clean toilets, or file letters. Somebody who had changed eleven trillion diapers had no standards left about great jobs. She could put a life back together.

Everybody cooed over the twins. "Look at their pretty curls!" people would cry. "Oooooh, I could just take you home with me!" women would croon. "What adorable little sweetie-pies!"

They're not adorable! thought Roo. I hate being a mother. I hate having twins. I hate being poor. I hate being bored. I hate having television for my only friend.

Momentarily she hated Diana, too, this complete stranger wielding a forest-green crayon.

"Ooooh, are those your babies? Are they

twins?" cried Diana. She waved at Val. "What's her name?" said Diana, in that wildly excited voice of a woman who was not the mother, who did not have to change the diapers and get up in the night to stop the crying. Justice required that this girl Diana should have to adopt Val and Cal.

"Valerie. And the boy is Callum."

"I love those names!" Diana waved again at the twins and to Roo's surprise, Val attempted to wave back, curling and tucking her fist, struggling to get it right.

Roo planned her escape from drudgery. Should she go back to the apartment for clothes? Briefly Roo wondered what her mother, her former classmates and teachers, her parents' neighbors, and the mothers and fathers of her old friends, would think of her. First an unmarried mother at sixteen and then living in the slums on welfare and then abandoning the children.

Who cares what they think of me? They don't visit me, do they? They don't phone me, do they?

Roo wanted to be a child herself so much she was perilously close to tears. She wanted somebody to take care of her, instead of her having to take care of them. She hated taking care of anybody. It was hard and no fun.

I want to be loved! she thought.

THE WAITING ROOM
7:51 P.M.

Diana's mother had rarely discussed Daddy.

Daddy. What a loving, affectionate word it was. And how affectionate the word still made her feel! After all these years, with no Daddy anywhere of any kind — and still, the word *Daddy* brought on a rush of lovely memory.

She could remember a lap and a raspy cheek.

She could remember a jacket, soft and gray, under which she had burrowed.

She could remember walking down a city street, holding his hand, could remember how his fingers tightened on hers at the crossings and how he swung her aloft to stand on the granite rim of a statue base; a statue, she thought, of a horse.

She could remember a car, sitting on pillows so she was high enough for the seatbelt, the radio playing, her father smoking a cigarette, and the windows open so the smoke would not enter her lungs.

She could remember one Christmas with Daddy. They had had a new chain of gold stars, which she and Daddy draped perfectly, so it glittered in the lamplight.

Diana's mother had never said bad things about Daddy. But she never said good things about Daddy, either. Daddy had turned himself into an unoccupied apartment. A dusty, musty unused space.

THE TRAUMA ROOM
7:50 P.M.

"Okay," said Dr. Gold quietly. "No sense going on."

She stepped back from the boy on the stretcher. So did the young doctor helping her, the two nurses, and the aide. They stood for a moment looking down at the body of a teenager who a few hours before had been alive and laughing and flirting and full of life.

Dr. Gold peeled off her gloves and dropped them into the bloody waste container. Slowly she ran her thin fingers through her graying hair and slowly she let the air out of her lungs and the hope out of her heart.

You never wanted to accept that you had lost a kid. You wanted to put him back together again. But this kid had broken himself like an egg — like Humpty Dumpty — and all the king's horses and all the king's men and all the technology of the finest hospital in the City could not put Alexander Whitman together again.

The aide telephoned Transport.

Not all the patients Transport moved were alive. The boy would be transferred to yet another stretcher. An all-metal gurney, because he no longer needed a mattress. It would have a lid, rather like a casserole, so that people they passed in the halls need not realize that a dead boy lay on that stretcher.

The aide went into the hall and erased the name Whitman from the board. The janitors moved in with mops to remove Alec's blood from the floor, and the aide rolled into Trauma a freshly made-up bed for the next patient.

THE WAITING ROOM
7:52 P.M.

Barbie, of course, had been a nurse in this City for many years. She, too, knew the outline of a handgun in a pocket when she saw it. And she knew the reason for the no-visitors rule when there was a gunshot wound.

The white guy who claimed to be the black guy's brother fondled his pocket, caressing his gun through the shiny polyester of his ugly pants. His fingers flexed and his face softened in a contemplative smile as he stroked the gun.

The GSWs had given no names. If the white guy knew it was Tillotson who'd been shot, very likely it was he who had shot Tillotson.

Barbie estimated there were thirty people in the Waiting Room. That included a half dozen small children.

Wonderful.

There was more than one button behind the nurse's desk.

She pushed her other choice.

THE WAITING ROOM
7:53 P.M.

Anna Maria knew she had to get her brother and sister out of there. She also knew that Dunk recognized her, and knew she was terrified, and was enjoying it. So she had to do this very casually.

She could gather her brother and sister and just walk outside, but what if Dunk followed her? At least here she had the minimal protection of the hospital walls and the other people waiting.

To reach the rest of the hospital, the cafeteria and gift shop, and take one of the many exits in those wings, she'd literally have to step over Dunk's feet, and get him to move his feet so she could push the stroller past. He wouldn't. He'd be more likely to take the stroller, claiming to be Anna Maria's brother as well.

Next to the hall was a stairwell, but she did

not know where the stairs went or even if she could get the stroller up or down them.

The hallway to the treatment area was closed by huge glass doors that opened only if the nurse or secretary pushed the right button.

Anna Maria decided the bathroom was most likely. Little kids always had to go to the bathroom. It was perfectly reasonable for her and Yasmin and José to leave the crayoning table and walk to the bathroom. She whispered in Spanish to Yasmin, "We're going to the bathroom."

"You go," said Yasmin loudly. "I'm fine."

"We're all going," whispered Anna Maria, kicking her.

"Don't kick me!" yelled Yasmin.

She tried to whisper in Yasmin's ear, but Yasmin thought Anna Maria was going to make her stop coloring, and she was having too much fun. "Stay on your side, Anna Maria," said Yasmin furiously and she shifted her little tot chair right up next to Trouble.

THE WAITING ROOM
7:59 P.M.

People made hundreds of phone calls from the pay phones. Diana could not imagine whom they were talking to. How many calls did a person need to make from an emergency room? Diana colored. What was it about crayons that made a person feel safe and calm?

Mary was trying to interview an elderly Russian patient. The man lived in a boarding house and had been stabbed in the face with a fork by another boarder. He held a handkerchief over his cheek while he waited to see the doctor. He wasn't going to die because of four holes in his cheeks, so he would wait a long time.

"I'm eighty-nine!" he cackled. "Been in America seventy-two years! My wife died forty years ago! I have five children. They're all dead!" He seemed quite proud of these facts.

"What is your address, sir?" said Mary patiently.

"None of your business."

"The doctor can't see you until you tell me your address, sir."

"Whaddaya wanna know my address for? Next thing you'll wanna know what boat I came on!"

Diana felt as if she were watching a video game.

Little windows of these people's lives opened when she clicked the screen. She would see them for a minute, or an hour, and she would know only what they had to tell: name, address, phone number, next of kin, insurance. They were bodies accompanied by a few facts and some pain.

She, Diana, was literally untouched by them. She would walk among them in her pink safety-zone jacket but she would do no suffering, answer no personal questions, pay no bills, see no doctors.

"None of your business!" shouted the Russian again. "Whaddaya wanna know my address for? Next thing you'll wanna know what boat I came on!"

The Waiting Room had lost its terror for Diana. In fact, there was a curious companionship to the place now, as if Diana and this group were boat people together, hoping to hang on long enough to reach shore.

And was one of the people here part of her own story?

Stepmother.

Never before had Diana let the word form in her mind.

If your father abandoned you, the woman he married was not your stepmother, only his wife. Mary had said *suppose we have fifty men named Williams here this year, we have to get the right one.* So this was not necessarily the right one.

I could look him up in the computer, thought Diana. That would spare me actually getting near him. What would I find in the computer? Date of birth, but do I know his date of birth? March, I think, but what year? Next of kin. Yes, that would be useful. It would give me Bunny's real name.

Diana never glanced at the young mother coloring next to her. Having babies when you were a teenager was so weird that Diana could not get into it. She knew she had nothing to say to such a person so she didn't try.

Right behind the crayoning table, two thin young men, extraordinarily well dressed compared to the rest of the waiting room, got to their feet. They shot their cuffs and synchronized watches, as if they were about to settle a business deal. They seemed almost giggly to Diana, who puzzled over it. Nobody else in an ER Waiting Room had anything to giggle about.

In the very back of the room slouched a

woman who was hugging her overcoat to her chest and eating Saltines. A surprising number of people were wearing coats in spite of the ghastly heat outdoors. Lots of them were also eating snacks. So there was nothing wrong with the woman having a snack. It was just that she was also eating the cellophane wrappers.

"Please tell me your address, sir," said Mary.

"None of your business!" shouted the Russian again. "Whaddaya wanna know my address for? Next thing you'll wanna know what boat I came on!"

Diana was beginning to see why he got stabbed with a fork.

"So what boat did you come on?" asked Mary, getting interested.

The woman eating the Saltine wrappers suddenly adjusted the bundle in her lap. It was not a coat. It was a blanket. Inside the blanket was a doll. The woman held the doll so that its head hung downward and its little neck splayed awkwardly on her legs.

Diana felt a chill of horror.

It was not a doll lying upside down on that lap.

THE THIRD HOUR

THE WAITING ROOM
8:01 P.M.

The woman's chin nodded down over the baby and then snapped up. She arched her torso vertically, sank back, and then, separately, her feet jittered around — her lower part dancing while her upper part slept.

Diana was deeply afraid. The woman was not behaving in an entirely human fashion. It was more as if that body were propelled by electrical impulses than by thought processes. And the baby was not lying there in an entirely human fashion, either. It was either dead or half dead. The woman belonged in the Psych Unit, but how did you get somebody in there? What did you do about a baby about to spill off a lap like a forgotten magazine?

Diana struggled to think clearly, but got nowhere, as if she were thinking inside pudding. If the baby's half dead, she said to herself, that's what the Emergency Room is for. To save the baby.

Diana looked around for help, but everybody seemed busy. From here she could see the ambulance bay outside, and it was filling with police cars. This seemed to be a police hobby — gathering, dispersing, gathering, dispersing. Barbie was conferring with Knika, both women half crouched behind the files, heads together, backs to the Waiting Room.

Diana was afraid the baby would go headfirst onto the floor. She left the crayoning table, accidentally bumping into the puffy men who were wending their way toward the exit. "Sorry," she muttered, steering around them. How did you mention to somebody that she was dropping her kid? "Ma'am?" she said finally. "May I help you?" She sounded more like somebody selling sweaters.

The woman continued to rock, shudder, and hold the baby downward. She tore open a Saltine pack and squirted the two crackers into her mouth by crushing the back of the pack. Cracker dust fell on the baby.

Diana sat down next to her and said loudly, "Have you seen the nurse yet?"

The woman looked up. Her eyes were so out of focus they didn't match each other.

Diana swallowed in fear. The fear did not go down but began filling her mouth and nose and eyes like some noxious gas. Diana knotted her own hands to stop herself from touching the woman. I'm afraid to touch her, thought Diana. Do I actually believe in the evil eye? "Let's have the nurse look at the baby," she said very loudly.

Now the Waiting Room stared at Diana with odd intensity, as if it were Diana behaving like a weirdo. Even the two puffy men stared at her, as if she had done something in very poor taste, knew nothing of Emergency Room etiquette.

They don't think I should shout, thought Diana. Just because she's nuts doesn't mean she's deaf. But I don't think anything will register in this woman unless I do yell.

Diana was grateful for the practice on drunks. Yelling was not as uncomfortable as it had been. "Let's go over to the nurse and ask her to look at the baby!" she shouted.

The crazy woman nodded away. It was more of a bobbing action than a head action and, with each move, the baby's head dipped lower and lower toward the floor. "He don't smile no more," she told Diana. "He not bright-eyed. So I come in."

Diana was desperate for help. She looked Barbie's way, ready to give her hand signals or something. Surely Barbie had heard Diana bellowing.

Barbie stood at her desk, which was unusual. Barbie, like Meggie and Knika, preferred to stay seated. But the look she shot Diana was truly exasperated. It was another of those *you stupid college volunteer!* looks. Diana wanted to cry. She knew she was doing the right thing to interfere with this crazy woman.

A security guard wandered over, passing slowly between the crayoning table and the men who seemed so excessively annoyed that Diana had banged into them. As if they were God, and nobody stepped on their feet. The pathetic security guard looked at nobody, just shuffled toward Diana as if he knew he was of no use. At least he was coming. What kind of Emergency Room was this, where they couldn't even respond to an emergency?

The guard's hand rested very lightly on Diana's shoulder. He was black, but his hand was white. In the split second before she realized he was gloved, she could not think how this division might have happened. It was just one more fearsome thing in an inexplicable situation. "Glove up," said the guard softly.

Diana pulled gloves out of her pocket. She had meant to give them to the children at the crayoning table, so they could play doctor, or blow the gloves up to make balloons.

To her amazement, Barbie — who never left her desk; patients had to go to her; she didn't come to them — was now beside them. "You did exactly the right thing," said the nurse. Diana was thrilled until she realized that Barbie was not talking to her; Barbie couldn't care less about the volunteer; she was talking to the woman. "Let's just unwrap this blanket," said the Admitting Nurse, "and — "

"Don't touch my baby."

Barbie's voice was melodious and soothing. She sure never talked to Diana that way. "Okay. You hold the baby. I'm just going to take the baby's temperature while you're holding him, okay?"

The woman rocked and twitched, grabbing another snack, plucking at the baby's wrappings, one foot dancing by itself around the chair leg.

Diana could not imagine what horrible disease the mother had.

The baby's eyes opened. It was alive, thank God.

"Now what we'll do is," said Barbie comfortingly, "you and I will go to the doctor, too, because you don't look like you feel too well either. Diana here's gonna hold the baby for you."

Diana had never held a little teeny baby in her life. She was as afraid to take the baby as she had been of approaching the mother. How do I support its neck? What if I drop it? What if —

But Barbie had already coaxed the baby out of the mother's arms and was putting it in Diana's. It did not feel like a real baby. It felt as light and unmoving as a doll. She pretended it was a doll and weirdly, after all these years, she could remember feeding her bedroom full of dollies, the ones that talked and wet.

Murmuring gently, the nurse got the mother to walk on through the Waiting Room with her, heading through the thick glass doors into the treatment area. Diana sat in a panic with her arms like sticks, not supporting the baby a whole lot better than the crazy woman had.

A black woman waiting for her son's leg to be set (he'd broken it in baseball practice) slid over from three seats away. "Honey. Hold that young'un like this." She moved Diana's hands into a better position, and then the baby lay against her chest more comfortably. Diana relaxed a little. "That mama's gonzo," said her rescuer. "Wonder what she's on."

Drugs! thought Diana, feeling both innocent and stupid. She had thought only of disease.

"She's *not* on 'em," said another woman, turning around to face them from two rows over. "That's the problem. She coming down *off* 'em."

The whole Waiting Room had been in on this soap opera. How weird. They had simply watched, as if it were TV, or a video game.

"She knew the baby needed a doctor, though," said Diana's helper. "I give her credit. The mama needs a fix but first she gets here to the ER so they see her baby."

Diana stared down into the baby's quiet little face. Your mama's an addict who eats cellophane, she thought. What chance do you have?

In the corner of her eye, she saw a whole raft of police coming through the weather lock and telephone area.

A male nurse came out to take the baby to the pediatric ER. "Good, you're gloved," he said.

"Why did I have to glove?"

"Addicts mostly are HIV positive," he said. "So probably her baby is, too." Gently he scooped the baby into his arms. He held the child — they didn't know yet whether it was a boy or a girl — and rocked it. He talked to the baby as he walked away, cuddling and nestling the tiny person the way the mother had not been able to. "Let's get you fixed up, sweetheart." He kissed its tiny forehead and snuggled the baby up to him as if it were his own.

But right now, the baby *is* his, thought Diana, and she was filled with awe. *He loves that baby.* I want to be a good person like that. I want to love other people's babies instead of being scared of them. Diana stared at her gloved hands.

"Don't worry," said her friend. "You can't get AIDS holding the baby. You'd have to share needles with the mama. You're safe."

Diana's eyes suddenly filled with tears. She

felt like a little girl, not a college woman. "But what will happen to the baby?"

The black woman put a gentle arm around Diana's shoulder and said nothing.

They both knew what would happen to the baby.

It would die.

THE EMERGENCY ROOM
8:01 P.M.

"This place is such a zoo," said the angry couple. They had been taken to a treatment room, but nobody had ever come to administer any treatment, or even to *look* at their son. Back and forth they stalked in the tiny room, seething with fury. If there had been anybody to hit, they would have gotten into fistfights. But there was only Seth, and the color of the pink jacket told them Seth was nobody and could accomplish nothing.

"I hate this place!" hissed the mother. "This disgusting zoo with these incompetent people!"

Seth heard this constantly. "What a zoo," people would say, as the flow and ebb of patients and professionals passed them by. "Is it always like this?" they would ask Seth, their lips curled in anger and shock.

Sometimes they didn't call it a zoo, but instead talked about how they hated this place. "I hate this hospital," people said many times every night. "I hate everybody in it. They make you wait; they're no good; they don't know what they're doing; it's too crowded and it costs too much."

Sure enough the mother brushed tears from her cheeks and said in a high-pitched, nearly hysterical voice, "If I had known what a zoo it was going to be, I wouldn't have come."

She had had to come. Her son was in such bad shape she had had no choice, and she knew it. Eventually, he would get the attention he needed, but the doctors weren't free right now. That was that. But nobody could stand the idea that their child didn't come first. Especially when their child was as desperate as this one.

"I hate this place," agreed the father.

Only the son said nothing. How could he? The pain and fear must have been unbearable. He just sat very still on the edge of the stretcher, feet hanging down, holding his mother's hand. He was about twelve. Seth had never even been hurt, let alone experienced anything like what this kid was going through. Would he have been this brave when he was in sixth grade?

The father moved into the hall to do some more swearing, as if four-letter words would bring a doctor on the run. By now Seth knew that doctors really didn't hear anything like that; their patient load was so heavy, and they had so many other worries, that the swearing and the anger just blended into the general chaos.

Seth never knew what to say when people swore at the hospital. He loved this place. He loved everything about it, but most of all, actually, he loved the zoo-ness. So much to see and stare at and learn from! And although it probably was a mean and low comparison, there *was* something zoo-y about the patients on display in their many cubicles. Curtains instead of bars, doctors instead of keepers. It was a teaching hospital, and the patients really were exhibits.

Sure enough, the medical students who a moment ago had been in the Family Room finding out how to tell elderly parents that their thirty-year-old son was permanently comatose, now gathered at the door of the Ophthalmologic Room. Gently maneuvering the parents out of their way, the specialist and the Attending began to lecture. "And this is an avulsed eyeball from a tumor. . . ."

This. A terrified twelve-year-old whose brain tumor was pushing his eye right out of his head. *This* — his sobbing mother and his stunned father. Here, they were just people to shift over to make room for the medical students. *This* was just an eyeball. In this inner-city ER, there was no such thing as bedside manner. You counted yourself lucky to have a doctor reach the bedside at all.

The very pretty medical student leaned over the boy, examining him with a sort of fascinated greed. Then she shifted, letting the nerdy one with the glasses have his turn. Nobody spoke to the boy, nor to his parents. They were concerned only with the eyeball. This time Seth had to agree when the mother whispered, "I hate this place," and the father added, "It's such a zoo."

Seth wanted to tell them, "But even if we are a zoo, we'll save your son!" But he could not, because he did not know if anybody or anything could save their son.

Half wanting to catch the pretty woman's eye — see if he rated an air kiss again — and half wanting to hear everything the Attending said, Seth slid into the lineup.

The Attending gave Seth a look of pure annoyance. "We're busy here," he said coldly. "Go find an errand to run."

I hate them, too, thought Seth. A flush rose up on his face as he stumbled past the pretty doctor. She never glanced at him. Had she forgotten him? Did the pink jacket really turn him into so much volunteer wallpaper? Or was she, too, irked that he was taking up valuable floor space?

He was deeply glad he had not tried to fake

being a medical student; that particular Attending would have called the police.

He glanced into the cubicle where Robert Searle lay.

The space was empty. No bed at all, which meant the patient had been rolled to X-ray, or CAT scan, or Operating Room, or possibly admitted to a regular floor in the hospital. Had Diana ever spoken to him? Or even walked into the room just to look at the guy?

He tried to imagine himself doing nothing in such a situation. Was not investigating a girl kind of reaction? Or an abandoned child reaction? Was Diana being very mature or very juvenile?

He stared at the empty room. Many times in Seth's childhood he had wished his father would disappear. His father had had such high standards: Whether it was soccer or algebra, doing dishes or writing term papers, Seth's father expected the best. He had always been on Seth's case, hounding, nagging, tutoring, working alongside.

In fact, on the September day Seth flew to college, the best thing had been leaving his father seven hundred miles away.

He was stunned to find his eyes filling with tears. He who never cried. He who could not cry even if it was an assignment, like that weird time in psychology class when the professor actually required crying to see who could do it on demand. Most of the girls could. Most of the boys could not.

Oh, Dad! thought Seth, his eyes spilling like his heart.

He had a father who had never skipped a birthday or a Christmas, that was for sure. A father who never skipped dinner or breakfast either. A father who was so *there* that Seth had had hideouts to avoid him.

"Volunteer!" yelled Meggie.

Seth brushed his face on his sleeve and walked blindly toward Meggie. He would telephone Dad tonight. He had never told his parents about his ER volunteering, although they would be very proud. His parents had orchestrated so much of his life that Seth had opted for privacy on his choices at college. He could no longer imagine why. He had parents who wanted to know! He was three hundred sixty-five days times many years luckier than Diana.

"Volunteer." A nurse called out. "Take this patient up to seven three."

The patient was nine years old, an adorable little pigtailed child who looked and acted as healthy as Seth. Healthier. The mother, on the other hand, was acting as if the little girl were on her deathbed, wringing her hands, hyperventilating, begging the nurse to accompany them. "You'll be fine," said the nurse, walking away.

"I hate this hospital!" muttered the mother, right on cue.

Seth could not imagine why the child was being admitted. Any fool could see there was nothing wrong. He collected the chart and set out for seven three, the mother whining, and the little girl — by hospital rule in a wheelchair — bouncing and chattering.

"Asthma," explained the mother, spitting out the words with wrath. "We were here all last night because Mandy had such a severe attack, but they sent us home." The mother made this sound like a staff crime that ought to be punishable by death. "Then Mandy had another attack this afternoon, which of course wouldn't have happened if anybody in this zoo had even a pea-sized brain and admitted her back last night. I knew they had to admit her! But would they listen to me, her mother? Oh, no! Not those arrogant worthless doctors! So of course she has another attack, and they act as if it's my fault, but this time they told us we wouldn't have a second chance."

No second chance? Was that a euphemism for dying? Couldn't be. Plain old wheezing couldn't kill a healthy little girl. No way. The mom was an hysteric. "She looks fine now," he said.

"It's temporary. They gave her oxygen and

medication. Hurry up." The mother tugged at Seth's jacket and gave him a little push. "We have to get to the pediatric floor."

"It's true," Mandy told Seth. "I've been nearly dead twice now." She was as proud of this as the gunshot victim had been of his wound.

He would research asthma when he got back to the college library. Could you really die of asthma?

They got on the elevator. Seth punched 7, and up they went. Too late, he realized he had gotten on the wrong elevator. This was the way to CAT scan. There were four separate banks of elevators in the hospital. He was in a building that did have a seventh floor, but not the pediatric seventh floor. Were these buildings connected on any floor but ground level? Or should he just go back down and start over?

Seth hated being a confused amateur. He did not want this panicky mother to know they were on the wrong elevator.

They got off at 7.

He pushed the wheelchair forward to the nearest nursing desk where the secretary (Meggie's twin) said irritably, "Seven pediatric? You took the wrong elevator."

"Oh, my god!" shrieked the mother. "We aren't even in the right building? What if Mandy has an attack?"

"You can get there from here," said the secretary irritably. "It's just stupid, that's all. Go down that hall all the way to the end, take two lefts, going all the way to the end of each of those halls, and then a hard right at the third drinking fountain."

A ridiculously long hall stretched before them. What were they doing — crossing the state line? He pushed the wheelchair past dozens of doors.

"This is taking too long!" cried the mother. "Mandy, don't have an attack!" Now she was clutching at Seth's jacket and Mandy's sweater. *"Whatever you do, don't have an attack right now!"* she shrieked.

Mandy began to cry. Seth could hear her sucking breath in to accommodate the crying. Her chest sounded as if it were full of bubbly water.

"Oh my god," said the mother. "She's going to have an attack right now! And we don't have oxygen and all because they gave me some volunteer kid instead of a real person!"

Seth took the second left and prayed he would locate all three drinking fountains.

"You don't know what you're doing!" cried the mother. "Mandy, *don't have an attack.*"

Seth found the first drinking fountain, which was good because he was about to have an attack himself. Mandy was crying harder.

The mother launched herself at somebody in a uniform. "Where is pediatric seven?" she shrieked.

The janitor jerked a thumb in the direction Seth was already going but did not look up and said nothing.

"I hate this hospital," said the mother, striding on ahead. "I hate everybody in it. I hate the doctors and the nurses and the whole staff and every single stupid, worthless, uninformed volunteer. Mandy's going to have an attack right here, where we're completely lost and there's no oxygen."

Seth pushed the wheelchair faster and accidentally rammed the heavy metal footrests into the back of the mother's heels.

She screamed in pain, threatening to sue Seth and sue the hospital and sue the whole world.

"I'm sorry," said Seth desperately. "It was an accident, I'm really sorry, but here we are at the third drinking fountain." Except of course he could no longer remember whether to go left or right.

He paused, looking both ways, hoping for a sign that said PEDIATRICS. No. Nothing. This hospital believed you should have been born knowing where you were.

Having her mother turn into a basket case apparently satisfied Mandy. She stopped crying and pointed to an unexpected corridor that went sort of backward. There in the distance was the pediatric nursing desk.

The mother limped after Seth, cursing, while Seth whipped forward. He turned Mandy and her chart over to the nurse and fled, keeping his hand over his ID so that the mother would not know his name when she filed suit.

THE WAITING ROOM
8:01 P.M.

This Diana. You could tell from her haircut and her perfect makeup, the very slight flowery scent of her expensive perfume, the lovely tiny earrings which — knowing what college she went to — had to be real emeralds . . . you could tell that this girl Diana had everything and always would have everything.

Roo had half thought that maybe she and this Diana would talk about things like cheerleading and pompom squads. English papers and gym class. Boyfriends and hairstyles.

But Diana never looked her way.

Why should she? thought Roo. I've ruined my life. She doesn't want to catch it. I'm like a bad cold. Nobody wants to get near me.

Roo's brief plan to run away from home evaporated. How pathetic. She couldn't go anywhere. Mothers never got to go anywhere. Even if you were a drug addict and had AIDS, which meant you had two very consuming things to think about — your next fix and your death — you had to put your baby first and come to the Emergency Room.

Roo was even more jealous of Diana now — the way the black woman had comforted her.

Roo needed it more, she knew she did. Roo didn't have a mother who intended to comfort her; she had a mother who was going to go on scolding her forever; making her pay every possible price for dumb judgment.

The male nurse carried the little AIDS baby back to the Pediatric ER. He kissed the tiny forehead over and over and crooned in that singsongy voice people always used with Roo's twins. She had the odd thought that she would like to date a man like that. A man who sang to sick babies.

My babies aren't sick, she thought. They don't have AIDS. They're here on a pretense.

The door closed behind the nurse and the sick baby, and Roo was aware of a deep relief within herself.

Her babies were beautiful and healthy and quick to learn new things. People loved to snuggle her babies, and they loved to sing to her babies, but not to comfort them in terrible illness. Because they were beautiful and healthy and quick.

Roo turned to look at her own children. She needed to see them, solid and safe and strong, the way they had been born and the way she was raising them.

I'm raising them! thought Roo. I've pulled it off. It was stupid to get pregnant and it was even more stupid not to give the children up for adoption. But even so, stupid as I am, I've pulled it off.

She began remembering things — funny minutes, silly times, giggly afternoons, snuggly hours. Good things about these twins who were so relentlessly *there*.

All these memories swelled her heart in the short, short time it would take to swivel in her chair and see Callum and Valerie, asleep in their double stroller.

THE WAITING ROOM
8:06 P.M.

When the city police, rather than the security guards, strode through the great glass doors, it was different. In this terrible heat, the cops nevertheless wore all their layers. Uniform piled on uniform, hips enlarged from leather belt, pistol, stick, radio, gloves, keys. Their suits were dyed a deeper, stronger blue, as if they were also deeper and stronger cops.

Hands splayed below their waists, like western sheriffs about to grab for guns, their eyes surveyed the room. People shrank down, trying to look invisible, or at least ordinary. They lifted magazines before their faces, or carefully studied the television on the wall, or decided it was time to concentrate on filing their nails.

The cops separated slightly, forming a net.

They knew who they wanted.

For a moment the dealers radiated insolence. They could get away with anything, always had.

But Dunk's nerves clocked in, on the timer of his drug use. He could not meet the cops' eyes without blinking too much. Then his muscles blinked, too, and he was standing there twitching, and knew his impotence, and hated the cops and himself and every witness in the room.

THE WAITING ROOM
8:07 P.M.

"Now, sir," said the police, trying to be relaxing and firm and in control.

Ridiculous. The person in control was the person whose gun was out. Dunk. He was back in control and he knew it and he loved it . . . and he waved it around.

It looked like a squirt gun.

But Anna Maria knew dealers, and this was a dealer who had become an addict. Not a good sales plan. She knew the odd staring blaze in his eyes, the off-center confusion that would make him do anything without warning. She knew the gun would not squirt water.

Anna Maria prayed to the Lord Jesus not to let José cry or throw his bottle again. She had had her chance to run and she had screwed up. Nothing could be done now.

The thing was not to move. Like a little animal when a hawk flies overhead, the thing was to freeze, and not be seen.

The cops were also frozen. They saw the flutter in Dunk's brain and muscles and knew they were not dealing with sanity. Anna Maria saw the cops spreading their minds as well as their hands, trying to think about her and Yasmin and José and all the other kids in the Waiting Room at the same time they thought about armed dealers.

They didn't call it "hopped up" for nothing. The man with the gun was hopping around, his wires crossed so that his feet moved whether he meant them to or not.

Dunk kicked the double stroller.

Cal slept on, but Val awakened with a scream. It was the kind of scream that makes parents crazy; the kind of scream that turns a cute kid into the most annoying, obnoxious creature alive.

Dunk's nerves split like pieces of wire about to be spliced; he came apart at the sound of the screams and jerked Val out of the stroller to silence her.

The patients and families packed into the Waiting Room had a lot more to worry about now than just waiting. Waiting looked pretty good from here.

THE WAITING ROOM
8:08 P.M.

His hands were too full. He did not know what to do next and everybody knew it. He was going to drop something, either the baby or the gun. Or he was going to shoot somebody, either the baby or whoever else the gun happened to be pointing at. He wasn't aiming. He was just holding.

The cops needed to give him choices, help him figure out what to do with those arms that were too full. "Now, sir," said the police. "You don't wanna mess with no baby. Babies are a pain. Let's just put the baby back in the stroller and talk about this."

The other dealer had sat down. Carefully. He was as afraid of the gun as everybody else. He held himself pointedly, like a rocket about to blast into space and leave this mess behind.

Dunk had no secure grip on anything — not the gun, not the baby, and certainly not himself. He was about as hopped up right now as the mother eating the cracker packages. Fear and adrenalin had pushed him even farther than the drugs.

The baby he held under his arm like a newspaper flopped back and forth. It never stopped screaming, its sweet little face all peeled back like an orange into one great shriek.

The police had to shout over the baby's racket, just when they wanted to be all soothing and friendly.

"So, sir," they yelled, as if Dunk deserved a title of respect, as if when they thought of Dunk, they thought "sir."

Scum, thought Anna Maria. Very good thing Dunk had not grabbed José, who was a biter. If José had bitten a drug dealer, he would get shot.

The cute little teenage mother did not seem to fathom the situation. She got up from her toddler chair, and stood right between the pointed gun and the police. "May I have my baby please?" she said, like somebody from a suburb, like somebody wanting the grocery boy to get a can off a high shelf.

The gun and the hand holding it went back and forth as if Dunk were playing Ping-Pong. But it was no soft little white ball that would go bang.

The mother looked like a high school girl.

She dressed the way Anna Maria wanted to dress when she was in high school. She held out her arms as if she actually thought Dunk would just give her her baby back.

Dunk stepped back, and then stepped back again. Anybody would have shifted anyplace for him, but people were sitting down and had nowhere to go. He pressed up against the black woman whose son had the broken bone.

Any semblance of control and power had vanished. Whatever the drugs and the nervousness might be doing in Dunk's system, they had turned him into total panic; total consuming panic.

"Now let's not get all excited here," said one of the cops. He was trying to keep his voice slow, but he had as much adrenalin pumping in him as the dealer, and his voice ripped as frantically across the room as the baby's. "Let's just not get ourselves all worked up."

This was absurd. The cops and the dealers were so worked up now they were practically on the ceiling.

The cop edged forward. "You wanna let me hold the baby? How about you let me hold the baby?"

Yet again, Diana listened to somebody tell somebody else where to go. It seemed to be an Emergency Room favorite, this sentence, consigning people to hell. It struck Diana that the creep holding the baby, like the girl in CIU, already lived there.

The dialogue did not sound like anything in a movie. The cops forced themselves to back off physically. They were panting, as if they had been working out in the gym for hours, been on the StairMaster and the treadmill and lifted weights. All they had done was face a gun for a few seconds.

None of the cops did much. One of them actually took a pack of Juicy Fruit gum and opened a stick for himself, chewing noisily. "Want a stick of gum?" he said to the guy with the baby.

Gum? thought Diana incredulously.

The ploy worked, unfortunately, with the wrong person.

"I do," said Yasmin, getting up.

Yasmin loved gum. She, too, walked right between the gun and the police. The cop gave the Juicy Fruit to her, smiling as if this was what he had had in mind. "Honey, you go sit over by the nurse, okay?"

THE WAITING ROOM
8:12 P.M.

Anna Maria could tell the cops hated having kids around. It terrified them that they could not protect the kids; that the most likely to get hurt, as always, were the smallest and weakest.

Yasmin went over by the nurse, where she was scooped up and removed. Good. Anna Maria's only responsibility now was José. She was sorry about the baby girl, but Val was not her problem.

The police tried to talk the gunman into setting the baby down.

They tried to talk the young mother into backing off.

They tried to talk the dealer into getting his buddy to hand over the gun and the baby.

The other dealer claimed he'd never seen the guy in his life.

Dunk's eyes, flared wide with terror, flew

toward Anna Maria, and she realized that she was the only one in the room who could actually name him.

Well, she wasn't dying that way.

In school tomorrow they had Art, and Anna Maria loved Art. She would take her crayon drawing in to show the Art teacher. He had promised they would make papier-mâché, and Anna Maria thought those were such pretty words: papier-mâché. What pretty things would they make out of papier-mâché?

Dunk began backing up again, waving his weapon.

He was going to get himself pinned in the narrow corridor at the back of the Waiting Room.

That was fine with Anna Maria. She would grab the stroller, go out the other way, grab Yasmin, and beat it for home.

The gun went off, tossing its hot shell back against the baby's back while the bullet itself spun harmlessly across the room. The baby girl screamed horrifically when she felt the burn. The whole Waiting Room took this as a signal to start screaming, and the place erupted in howls of fear, one of which, Anna Maria was sure, was Dunk's own scream.

But he had the baby, and nothing else mattered.

He leaped backward down the corridor, ripped open the door that said STAIRS and was gone. The police launched themselves after him, yelling into their walkie-talkies, bumping into each other and leaping over sprawled legs. As television went, it looked more like a football game than a cop show.

THE WAITING ROOM
8:13 P.M.

The bullet had gone into the wall.

The boy whose leg was broken said, "Woooooooo! Ma, let's dig it out! I want it for a souvenir."

"Boy, you crazy," said his mother. She was fanning herself with exhaustion and relief that the gunman was out of the room. Her son hobbled over, disregarding his pain, and used his penknife to dig out the bullet.

"Don't do that," said a grumpy patient. "The police will need that for the trial."

Street-smart people laughed. "Ain't never gonna be no trial. That man, he got off before, he get off now."

The young mother scooped up her remaining baby, staring at her little son with wonder; as if they had never met; as if the baby were some strange and wondrous creature from Mars.

The volunteer sat with her jaw hanging open, as if she had never seen anything like this in her life.

Anna Maria grabbed the stroller and beat it.

THE WAITING ROOM
8:19 P.M.

My baby girl, thought Roo.

She could not move. She could not even go to hold Cal.

I'm no good, she thought. A good mother would run after him, screaming and beating on him. A good mother would shoot him dead or break his kneecaps.

She tried to figure out who in this Waiting Room was a good mother. That addict, coming down, her whole body and mind collapsing into one big, trembling, chaotic mess? But who knew enough to know her baby needed a doctor? Was she a good mother?

No.

Nobody that far gone could be a good mother.

But she loves him, thought Roo. *She loves him.*

Roo was swamped with needing love: needing to see it, needing to feel it. Needing to hold the two people on earth who loved her: Callum and Valerie.

I forgot that part of it, thought Roo. They love me. No matter how much they drive *me* crazy, I don't drive *them* crazy. They go right on loving me. There is plenty of love in my house.

She found that she had peeled Cal out of the stroller, and draped him on her shoulder where he lay in that heavy clingy way that babies had, melding right onto Roo, his little hot cheeks one with her neck.

She found that she was sobbing, but not talking.

She found that the police were telling everybody to stay calm, especially her.

She found that the black woman was pulling her down. "Here, honey, here's what we'll do," said the woman. "You hold your little one, and I'll hold you, and we'll wait, and I just know the other baby will be fine." Roo lay deep inside the blessed comfort of somebody else's hug. Somebody else's unjudging love. "Just fine," said the woman. Singsongy, crooning a lulla-bye. To Roo. "Ju-uu-st fine," she repeated, rocking and comforting.

CITY HOSPITAL:
SUBBASEMENT
8:21 P.M.

Seth took the stairs down from seven, for no reason except the pounding of his hard shoes on the hard stair treads seemed to empty some of his embarrassment. Instead of walking through the public areas of the hospital to get back to the ER, he would take the tunnels.

Of course, now when he was angry and felt stupid, he ran into three men who remembered him — they were in patient transport — and said, "Hey, man. How ya doin'?" and he in return had to say, "Not bad, man. Gonna live."

They slapped palms and slouched on.

Seth did not actually feel as if he were going to live. He felt supremely stupid, and it was a feeling Seth rarely had. What with Diana rubbing him as raw as the pavement had rubbed that kid on the bike, and his being a total uncoordinated jerk with that asthma mother —

Seth wanted to go to the gym and hit a punching bag about seven hundred times.

He hit the bottom of the stairs and turned into the yellow tunnel.

He had done something wrong.

The tile in this tunnel was pea green.

Hmmm, thought Seth.

He could have walked back up a flight, come out on the ground floor, and found his way back. But this was his chance to trace another underground route. He was delighted. He knew by now that the volunteer jacket was amazing protection. Not only would nobody forbid him to go places, but they would guide him, because even though volunteers were pesky, they were also absolutely necessary. No hospital could manage without the volunteers.

Although, thought Seth, the asthma mom could probably have managed a lot better. Well, forget her, so she had sore ankles and sued the place. She didn't know his name, did she?

Seth followed the tunnel.

He was thrilled to pass a door (no lights on within) that read PATHOLOGY LAB. He was even more thrilled to pass a door (you couldn't see in this one) that said MORGUE. Each of those doors was not simply locked, but also padlocked.

At the next turn, he passed the underground

security station, where narcotics prescription sheets were kept and an officer sat twenty-four hours a day keying people in and out. Inside were security cameras focussed on every entrance to the hospital. Seth waved at the guard, who frowned at him but didn't question him.

Seth loved it.

In another hundred paces, he came to a choice. The pea-green tunnel intersected with the yellow tunnel. Now. Should he follow the yellow, which would take him back to the ER, or explore the green, which would not?

Seth deliberated.

He wanted the new territory but, on the other hand, he was starving to death and Diana might have supper with him if he begged and pleaded and pointed out that he was now in a position to blackmail her about Bed 8. Or even interrogate Bed 8 for her.

Which I might do anyway, he thought.

There's no law against it. I could just sashay up to Bed 8 and say, "Why, Mr. Searle, I know a girl who looks so much like you! Do you have a daughter Diana?"

Then if the guy died of a heart attack, Seth would know that yes, the guy had a daughter Diana.

Seth took the yellow tunnel and entertained himself by bouncing up and down, sticking his fingers up inside the morass of wires and ducts and pipes that comprised the open ceiling. If this were TV, he thought longingly, I'd find an opening in that air-conditioning duct and crawl along it till I found the opening over Bed 8, and I'd drop on top of him and crush the evidence out of him.

With this happy thought, Seth bumped into a man carrying a baby and a gun.

EMERGENCY ROOM
8:27 P.M.

The cops redistributed the people in the Waiting Room, thrusting them here and there for their own safety or the cops' freedom of movement.

Diana was pushed behind Knika's heavy glass enclosure, and from the safety of that bulletproof place she stared. It was a zoo, and she had a ticket for the show.

The police threw the other dealer against the floor, knotting his wrists behind him so quickly that Diana realized the man on the floor had done this before and was cooperating. Didn't want his elbows snapped. Knew perfectly well he wasn't going anywhere.

"Wudn't me, man," the guy kept saying, his mouth plastered against the filthy linoleum of the Waiting Room. "Not my idea, I din' take no kid."

"What's his name, the guy who did? What do we call him?"

"Dunk. His name Dunk."

"What's his real name?"

"Kevin Duncan."

Kevin Duncan. It sounded like somebody you would know from high school. Somebody who would sit across from you in biology or on the bench during basketball games. Maybe he had. Drug dealers were kids once.

But not for long.

How different the Waiting Room seemed now. She was suddenly incredibly afraid. The room seemed to be percolating with evil — people actually willing to kill people, turn them into addicts, kick them when they were down, bring them down if they weren't there yet. Disease, too, percolating like coffee. Not interesting things; not things to be fascinated by and learned from; but things equally evil and prepared to kill: AIDS. Tuberculosis. Hepatitis.

Knika's intercom said loudly, "Volunteer to Treatment Desk."

Meggie. Meggie actually wanted a volunteer back there. Didn't she understand that there was a hostage situation in the Waiting Room? Diana shook her head. Really, Meggie was such a fool.

Knika said, "Well? They need you."

"But Knika — "

"What're you gonna get done here? Huh?"

"Well — well — I'm — "

"You're going to watch the show. I don't blame you. It's one of the perks of working in the ER. Aisle seats."

Diana had known that she volunteered in order to have an aisle seat for the show, but somehow she had not realized that the regular staff did, too. She had thought they were just clerks, just typing up their little insurance garbage. She flushed. None of them were "just" clerks. They wouldn't be here, putting up with all this, enduring all this, if they didn't think it mattered, didn't want to be part of it.

After a while Knika said, "They probably do need you back there."

Diana took a long last look at the ER.

Police blocked the stair exit.

Police had moved the other dealer to the holding room.

Police arrived, car after car, in the parking turnaround.

The little mother, so pretty, so young, so stunned, lay like a sick child herself in that grown-up mother's arms. They looked like three generations: grandma, mother, grandson.

Television arrived: The amazingly bright lights and gaudy truck of Channel 8 drove right onto the sidewalk (where any unfortunate sick person would receive a ticket or even get towed), and the reporting staff and cameramen leaped out and ran to the ER entrance.

Maddeningly, Meggie's voice, dry and cynical came on the intercom again. "We featuring any volunteers tonight? They go for supper? They trying to be interviewed on TV?"

Supper, thought Diana, abruptly pierced by fierce hunger. She had not had a single moment to think about supper.

Well, she didn't have time now. She kept having to prove to Meggie that just because she was a college freshman didn't mean she was worthless. She touched Knika's shoulder, for what reason she really didn't know — some kind of communication she needed to make — and Knika patted her hand as if Knika, at least, knew.

Diana went back to Meggie.

"We got a patient up at Radiology they need to move back down," said Meggie. "You know where Radiology is?"

"Yes."

"Patient's name is Searle. He goes back in Bed Eight."

The guy shot at him.

Luckily Seth was standing so close and the man was so rattled that the gun shot way down the tunnel and the single bullet ricocheted a hundred feet away. "It's only me!" said Seth quickly, trying to look harmless and dull. "No need to shoot! I'm a friend!" He was mostly relieved he hadn't wet his pants. The volunteer jacket didn't hang low enough to hide that.

The man waved the gun.

The baby screamed.

"He needs his diaper changed," said Seth, who would not have known a diaper if he sat in one. "Why don't you let me do that?"

"Which way out?" said the guy.

"Turn right down that green tunnel," said Seth, pointing. "Takes you right out." And past the police bay, but no need for details.

The man nodded, handing over the baby and racing for the green tunnel.

Seth stared at him.

The whole exchange had been so fast that Seth really had not got the faintest idea what had happened. He only knew that some really hopped-up druggie whose eyeballs were practically spurting out of his head had just handed him a little kid.

It seemed like the kind of situation that Barbie would know how to handle, so Seth headed for the ER while the baby screamed on in his arms. The kid had lungs. Whatever other problems this baby had, it hadn't come into the ER for asthma.

Seth reached the bottom of the stairs only to have the heavy metal door thrown open by what looked like fifty cops, as hopped up as the druggie, but on adrenalin. Their guns were also pulled but they probably had more training and better aim than the druggie.

Seth could think of no syllable, no movement, no nothing, that had prepared him for this.

They stared at each other for a moment, the panting, insanely aroused officers and the terrified college kid.

Seth pasted his handy all-purpose smile on his face. "Hi, I'm just a volunteer," he said. "Guy handed me this kid and headed down the green tunnel."

All the police but one shoved on past and thundered toward the green tunnel.

They were going to use their guns if it killed them, which it might. Seth and the remaining cop went into the stairwell, shut the door firmly against any kind of armed warfare, and Seth said, "So what's going down?"

The baby, whose lungs were getting a class-A workout, kept shrieking.

EMERGENCY ROOM
8:43 P.M.

"What do you mean, we can't go in there?" Susan and Mai were absolutely outraged. Who were these people attempting to block their entrance to the Emergency Room?

"We've got a little problem here tonight," said the policeman, "and we're not encouraging visitors."

"We don't need encouragement," said Susan. "We're here, and it's necessary, and you are not within your rights to prevent access."

"Am I within my rights to save your little life from a druggie gunman?" asked the cop.

"It looks as if you are completely unable to keep that sort of thing under control," snapped Susan. "My roommate was shot this evening. Where were you then?"

The cop looked interested. "Your roommate was the one who walked into the drug deal and got herself pasted?"

"Pasted?" whispered Mai. "Does that mean dead?"

"I haven't heard anything lately," said the cop. "She was alive when they brought her in."

"Excuse us," said Susan sharply, pushing her way forward. "We have to see her."

The cops looked at each other and then shrugged.

Susan and Mai charged into the Waiting Room. They took one look at the collection of pathetic human beings lining the walls and headed for the nurse, who did not look terribly impressive either. Obese. Probably smoked. Definitely not a vegetarian.

"How may I help you?" said the fat nurse, reaching for a patient form.

"We need to see our roommate, Jersey MacAfee. She was shot. She'll need us."

The nurse shook her head. "No visitors."

"You don't understand," said Susan. She hated dealing with stupid people. "We are her roommates and we have to be with her."

"No visitors," said the nurse. "We've got extraordinary problems this evening."

Susan was furious. She explained that her father was a lawyer.

The nurse replied that *her* father was also a lawyer and so what?

The Waiting Room enjoyed this immensely. It was always nice to have a chance to put one of these college kids in her place. The nurse enjoyed it, too. It was one of the perks of the ER, along with aisle seats. When people were obnoxious and pushy, you got to be *more* obnoxious and pushy.

Susan had met her match in an Emergency Room Admitting Nurse.

Finally Knika took pity on Susan and Mai. "Your roommate isn't even in the ER anymore," she said. "She was admitted, and she's in the Intensive Care Unit up on nine. They definitely have no visitors, but you can use this phone to call the charge nurse there and get some information.

EMERGENCY ROOM
8:45 P.M.

Roo had never changed a diaper so willingly.

Every inch of Valerie's soaking little body looked incredibly beautiful to her mother. Val never enjoyed diaper changes and grabbed Roo's hands as always, thrusting them away and arching her back to prevent Roo from getting it done. Always, always, this infuriated Roo and made her want to smack Val.

Now she thought — Val's got personality. She isn't some bland little passive nobody who just lies around. She's mine. And she's tough. And she fights back.

And I love her.

In a queer way, she knew she was obligated to the criminal who had shown her there were two good things in her life. Valerie and Callum. She finished changing the baby and kissed Val's throat and face and hair the way the male nurse had kissed the AIDS baby.

Val giggled and grabbed at her mother's nose.

Roo moved back just far enough to prevent it, and Val burst into a smile so joyful, so delighted, that Roo suddenly knew something. Val had no words yet, but she had thoughts, and the thought was — there's Mommy! My Mommy! My wonderful Mommy!

Roo carried Val back to the Waiting Room, where her new friend was rocking Cal. She put them both in the double stroller and called a taxi. "You gonna be okay for the night?" said the woman, frowning. "You got somebody to call? You don't wanna stay alone tonight, you hear me?"

Roo hugged her fiercely. "I have parents," she said. "They want me to live with them. I wouldn't because I've been so mad at them for being so mad at me."

"Boy, do I know how that feels," said the son with the broken leg. He was admiring his bullet. He tried to stuff it in his pocket before the nearest cop saw him, but he was too late. "Please can I keep my bullet?" he begged.

"Get a life," said the cop, holding out his hand.

Yasmin was with the social worker.

Anna Maria recognized him. Very tall, very thin, very black, very serious.

"Hi there," said the social worker, smiling down at her. "I'm Thomas."

Anna Maria said, "No English." She peeled Yasmin's hand out of the social worker's and said quickly in Spanish, "We're going home, Yasmin. He's trouble. Kick him if you have to."

The social worker said, also in Spanish, "No kicking. And you're not going home until I find out who you're with. You come here with your mother? Your grandmother? Your aunt? Who are you with? Who's sick?"

Anna Maria regarded the floor for a while. No fair when other people spoke Spanish.

The social worker had a little room with half-glass walls and he tried to take them in there. Anna Maria didn't move. Yasmin didn't move. José sucked on his bottle.

"Thomas!" said a nurse, grabbing him. "It's not enough we have a hostage situation going on here and television crews coming in. We've got a rape, you need to talk to her, and we've got a granny-dumping. Come on."

Thomas stared down from his great height at Anna Maria. She tightened her grip on the stroller and moved toward the exit. They were too busy here to bother with minor things, and she was minor. Thomas the social worker knew a thousand families where the kids brought themselves up, fed themselves, dressed themselves, got themselves to school. What was he supposed to do, adopt them all?

She showed her control by taking her family toward the door, marching like a matriarch of fifty, not a small child of eight. He let her go.

EMERGENCY ROOM
8:50 P.M.

Diana walked down the rear of the H-shaped ER.

She went down the corridor with the brown floor tile and turned right into the corridor with the gray floor tile. She pushed the up button for the Main Building's elevator. She waited. Eventually it came. She went to the third floor and turned right, and then right again. The hallways outside Radiology were always rather dim. She did not know if they were meant to be that way, to save the unfortunate waiting patients from having to squint upward at bright ceilings, or if they needed more bulbs.

There were three stretchers in the hall.

She went to the first one. It was a thin Asian woman.

She went to the second one. A grotesquely overweight human being whose gender was not immediately clear.

She went to the third one. A sleeping white man about fifty.

She stooped to read the wrist tag with his patient name and number. ROBERT SEARLE.

For a long time Diana Dervane stood at the head of that stretcher while the man slept on, not knowing that his daughter was there. As he had slept all these years, not knowing his daughter was anywhere.

I might have been Diana Searle, she thought. I might have sat in his lap and learned my multiplication tables. He might have taught me to play ball, or driven me to flute lessons, or applauded when I gave my first speech.

But I wasn't Diana Searle.

I was Diana Dervane.

And no matter who this is, he wasn't my father, was he? And never will be, will he?

She said to the sleeping stranger, "I'm going to roll your stretcher on back to the ER, sir. You don't have to wake up."

She thought about putting her ID in her pocket. No. She would not do that. If he woke, and read the tag, and if the name meant anything to him . . . or if he woke, and looked at her face, and saw something familiar . . . or if he did not wake, and so saw nothing, she would not get involved.

She would let happen whatever happened.

The man muttered a little when she accidentally bumped a corner, trying to shove the heavy stretcher toward the elevators. When the down elevator finally came, a resident standing inside it helped haul the stretcher into the elevator and helped shove it out again at the ground floor.

Diana normally flirted like mad with cute residents, or even plain residents. She didn't glance at this one. Didn't see that he had looked way past the repulsive pink jacket and appreciated the very pretty girl; that he would have liked to exchange names; meet her in the cafeteria.

She thanked him for holding the elevator door and pushed the stretcher on down to the empty space behind the beige curtain that hung around Space 8.

Why am I making this decision? Why am I letting go of it? And him?

Maybe, she thought, because he would ask what my life was like, and maybe it's no longer his business. Maybe I don't want to tell him how hard I worked and how much I cared about getting into this college. Maybe I don't want to talk about all the activities in which I excelled, the ones he never came to, never wondered about.

If it's him.

You'd think that at least I'd want to know if it's him.

But I don't.

EMERGENCY ROOM
8:55 P.M.

"I just wanted it to be more dramatic," said Seth.

"It was very dramatic!" cried Diana. She was filled with awe. She herself had been so afraid when the puffy creep took the baby that she could not possibly have done anything heroic. She had hardly even been able to go on breathing. "You were breathtaking, Seth! Imagine being so cool! Just taking the baby, ignoring the bullets!"

What Diana found breathtaking was that she had been so ignorant. She thought she knew what was going on in that Waiting Room; thought that after two hours she had a sense of the place. But she knew nothing. These people inhabited a world so different from hers that every conclusion she came to and every deduction she reached was wrong.

Like the security guards. They didn't sort

of drift and wander because they were half asleep. It was because they were wide-awake, and very careful; not wanting to start anything that didn't have to get started. She was the one who had not seen anything going on, who had barged into drug dealers, insulted them by not according them their due honor, and the guard had taken a major risk in crossing them also, to help her with the baby. She was the one to be rescued, not the rescuer. There was a certain amount of truth in the *you stupid college volunteer!* looks.

Okay, she thought. Next week I won't be so stupid. I promise.

She found it breathtaking that every event in the ER seemed to wipe out the previous one. She had actually not thought about the baby and the drug dealer when Meggie had set her on the road to Bed 8. She had not thought about the college girl who'd been shot, or the badly damaged motorcyclist, in hours.

She knew herself a little better than she had earlier in the day. Imagine accusing Seth of being calculating! Just who was calculating here, anyway? She herself had turned out to be a person who could calculate her own father right out of her life!

What Seth found breathtaking was that Diana was not going to find out whether Bed 8 was her father. How could she stand it? How would she ever sleep again, never mind tonight?

Diana was sent to get an emesis basin for a mother who wanted her baby to throw up neatly, a choice with which the nurses certainly agreed.

Seth slipped back into the computer section of Insurance. "Hi, Mary," he said. "Look up Searle for me, will you?"

Mary punched him in. Searle, Robert, had arrived at the ER at 1640 hours. 4:40 P.M. "What do you need?" she said to Seth, punching in the patient numbers to call up the screen that would hold the admitting information on Searle, Robert.

"I'm not sure." He knelt beside Mary and stared into the screen.

Robert Searle's DOB appeared. His birthplace: AMES, IOWA. His place of employment: EASTERN COMPUTERS. His wife's name: BERNICE. Was Bunny a logical nickname for Bernice?

Seth thanked Mary.

He stood at the edge of the Waiting Room, appearing trustworthy in his pink jacket. People felt comfortable with volunteers. Little did Bernice Searle know. He didn't let himself think about what he was doing. If Knika and Meggie and everybody else thought he was arrogant and interfering an hour ago, best they should not see him at his arrogant and interfering maximum.

He said, "Family with Mr. Searle?"

A woman got up quickly. She was very ordinary looking. He said, "Mr. Searle is back from Radiology. They still aren't letting visitors back, but I thought you'd like to know that progress is being made."

"Thank you," she said, trembling. "That's so kind of you. How does he look?"

"Fine," said Seth. "You look familiar. Is your name Bunny?"

The woman's jaw dropped. "Why yes," she said, smiling. The smile overtook her face and made her attractive, pleasant looking in a neighborly sort of way. "Where do we know each other from?"

He had forgotten to prepare an answer, but Knika saved him. "Volunteer! They need you in Trauma."

"Gotta run," said Seth.

"Of course," she said, looking confused.

Seth ran.

EMERGENCY ROOM
9:00 P.M.

They had been there three hours.

It felt like three hundred.

How did people work eight-hour shifts in this zoo?

Diana was more exhausted mentally and emotionally than she had ever been in her life.

How did medical students go through this — many more hours every day, every day in every week?

Did she want to be a doctor, and deal with so much pain?

Did she want to be a physician in an Emergency Room, where patients flew in and out, and you knew so little of who they were, and each remained a mystery, swiftly replaced by another?

She thought of the man with SOB, and how

in a previous life that meant son of a bitch but in this life it meant shortness of breath, and in any case, both fit Rob Searle.

"Volunteer to CIU," the loudspeaker paged. "Volunteer to Pedi. Volunteer to Admitting Nurse."

Seth, in the voice of one paging Earth to Daydreamer, said to Diana, "Volunteer to Volunteer."

She looked into his eyes. She had never bothered with that before. She had taken in the whole body, so to speak, and not tried for the windows to his thoughts. He looked softer, somehow. "Hey, Volunteer," she said to him. She touched him lightly, and the touch, fingertips to jacket, sent a shiver through them both.

When they enrolled as volunteers, they had had to sign promises not to walk back to the campus after dark. Taking a taxi was required. Diana thought of how big Seth was, how masculine, how ready to fight . . . and how meaningless that would be against a bullet. She thought Seth was a little less buttoned up than usual right now, and she herself — she was Jell-O. A taxi home? She wouldn't mind going on a stretcher, with a volunteer all her own to push her back to the dorm.

It dawned on her that if she really wanted one, she could definitely have a volunteer all her own.

Seth swallowed. Like the kid on the cycle, he went back for more. Who knew — maybe Diana wouldn't toss him to the pavement this time. "Want to go to the cafeteria before we get a taxi? I never had time for supper, did you? They're not serving hot meals anymore, but we could still get a sandwich."

She smiled and he tried to decide what the smile was: friendly or getting ready for the punch, and then she shook her head. Seth's heart sank. "I'm too tired to eat," Diana told him. That was the lamest excuse he'd ever heard. Fine, okay, she was too tired to — "Let's save dinner for a real date, Seth."

A real date? He didn't quite dare react to this.

"Volunteer to CIU," repeated the page. "Volunteer to Pedi."

Down the far hall came a new set of pink jackets; the late-shift pink jackets. Seth and Diana were done. They were off.

"Anything but a Monday, Seth, would be good," said Diana. "If every Monday is going to be like this, I never want to miss one."

Seth had lost interest in Mondays, his thoughts taking a familiar downward spiral. She was so beautiful. "Saturday?" he suggested, holding himself in till he saw whether she was serious. "A movie, too?"

"Saturday," said Diana. "Dinner and a

movie." She linked her pink-clad arm through his and looked back up at him and laughed. And this time, it was no air kiss.

In spite of the fact that in the last three hours Seth had worked on naked torn bodies and soppy babies and avulsed eyeballs and druggies coming off highs, he was embarrassed to be doing something as intimate as kissing in the hospital halls.

But he pulled it off.

Seth thought: *finally*. I'm eighteen, I'm at college, I can vote, I'm a grown-up . . . and I have a girlfriend.

Yes!

Seth and Diana left the Emergency Room. Hanging their pink jackets in the Volunteer closet, they signed out on their time sheets. When they left through the main entrance, a waiting taxi slid right up, whisking them back to the world of college dorms.

The world of a hurting city went on without them.

Agony and chaos, sorrow and fear. One person's story was replaced by another's in minutes.

Whatever day of the week a volunteer came to help, there would always be need.

About the Author

Caroline B. Cooney lives in a small seacoast village in Connecticut. She writes every day on a word processor and then goes for a long walk down the beach to figure out what she's going to write the following day. She's written over fifty books for young people, including, *The Party's Over*, *The Face on the Milk Carton Trilogy*, *Flight #116 Is Down*, *Flash Fire*, *Emergency Room*, *The Stranger*, and *Twins*.

Ms. Cooney reads as much as possible, and has three grown children.

CAROLINE B. COONEY

Caroline B. Cooney — Takes You To The Edge Of Your Seat!

BCE93349-7	Wanted!	$4.50
BCE45680-3	The Stranger	$4.50
BCE45780-3	Emergency Room	$4.50
BCE44479-5	Flight #116 Is Down	$4.50
BCE47478-9	Twins	$4.50

Available wherever you buy books, or use this order form.